DOGS

AND THEIR TWISTED TALES

AMY KRISTOFF

Deer Run Press
Cushing, Maine

Library of Congress Card Number: 2017902487

ISBN: 978-1-937869-06-9

First Printing, 2017, USA

Published by
Deer Run Press
8 Cushing Road
Cushing, ME 04563

Contents

DOGS

AND THEIR TWISTED TALES

A Dream or a New Reality?

He needed to clear his head after a horrible dream he'd had while taking an unanticipated Saturday afternoon nap. It was unanticipated because Jake never relaxed after driving his beloved 1967, powder blue Chevy Camaro. Unfailingly he would leave it parked outside the garage and basically stare at it when he wasn't wiping/dusting the interior. He hand-washed it later in the day, once the engine was cool.

This afternoon, all the concern Jake had had for his car the few years he'd owned it seemed trivial and stupid. However, he couldn't figure out what was affecting him more in that regard: the fact he'd hit a dog while out on his week-end drive; or the fact he'd dreamed there was revenge brought upon him for as much.

In his defense, the damned dog literally ran into his car! Right afterward, Jake parked and got out to investigate, admittedly initially only worried about his car. Fortunately it looked fine, but yes, there was a dead dog near the right rear wheel. Or he looked dead. What he found himself most focused on was the noticeable similarity between the dead dog's appearance and his dog Rags, his best friend growing up—but that wasn't initially the case. More on that later.

Anyway, Jake was taking a walk around the apartment complex where he'd been residing for the past three years. He was "enjoying" a smoke because he was so stressed out. He'd actually quit the habit shortly after moving in, since smoking wasn't allowed in the residential buildings. This was news to him because he'd failed to read all the fine print before signing the lease! So he also missed the paragraph regarding allowing one pet per unit, any size, as long as the pet was kept leashed and all waste was picked up. One day Jake happened to see a guy being dragged around by a black and white Great Dane and after finishing his cigarette, dashed back inside to read the entire lease.

As much as Jake loved dogs (despite any indication to the contrary), he refused to acquire one as long as he lived in an apartment. Hopefully the owner of the car repair shop where he worked would soon make good on his verbal promise to make Jake a partner, a reward for a dozen-plus years of "excellent work." Jake was a nobody but liked to think he was an above-average mechanic who deserved to have something good come of as much. Then he'd finally have some serious money to save and could eventually purchase a small farm like the ones he routinely passed when taking a weekend drive. However, none of those properties ever had a "for sale" sign in front. As much as he liked the area, there was something eerie about it. Maybe that had been part of its allure.

Jake had his brother, Rick, to thank for a lot of what he'd learned about cars – way before he had any formal education about them. Rick eventually took his know-how and fled to Phoenix, where he established a custom car conversion business, having wanted to leave boring Parker, Indiana, since he was a kid. Meanwhile, Jake felt like he was literally glued to this place, if only because he was born and raised here. Maybe at this point he didn't even want to leave. He felt like a dog finally let off the leash: so accustomed to a restraint there was no desire to stray.

Once Jake thought about it, why the hell would he make that comparison? He liked dogs, as mentioned, but he never made references to them, not like that, as in essentially including himself as one. It was bad enough he'd felt like an outsider his whole life, an alien even, as kooky as that sounded. Or everyone else was an alien, perhaps. (Which was more ridiculous?)

O.K., Jake was lighting another cigarette, having already finished the first one he'd smoked in three years. Obviously the desire to smoke never diminished, at least not for him. At this point it seemed like that was the least of his problems, especially since his smoking compulsion was only temporary. After all, he had the discipline to stop again – once he finished this pack.

One person who'd detested Jake's smoking habit was his ex-girlfriend, Louise. That made as good an excuse as any, explaining why she broke up with him. What bothered Jake most right now (next to how bothered he felt), was the realization he'd probably never again take a leisurely weekend drive on his favorite country road. It was questionable he could even handle another one of his drives, at least not in the near future. Given the fact it was only June, the summer was about to turn into a long one. With his luck, there'd be an Indian summer, and he'd otherwise be able to take "relaxing weekend drives" until Halloween, perhaps even past then.

If Jake hadn't invested so much time at "Bart's Auto Repair," he'd say a change was in order as far as scenery and everything else. With his brother in Phoenix, it was tempting to contact him about possibly working for him, at least temporarily.

Then again, that was a dumb idea! Jake wasn't even close to his brother, although Rick's second wife, Kelly, would send Jake a Christmas card. (It was obviously her handwriting.) The last time Jake spoke to his brother was right before he and Kelly moved to Phoenix. It was a "hello-good-bye" kind of phone call, and Rick made no secret of being in a hurry. At the time, Jake was already tallying up all the reasons his brother would be leaving the area – besides the fact Rick always hated living in the Midwest, let alone Indiana.

3

The first winter Rick and Kelly were in Arizona, Jake received a Christmas card from them that included a short note, inviting Jake to visit them "anytime." There was an address label on the envelope, and she'd written down their home phone, as well as Rick's new cell phone number, with a Phoenix area code.

It was impossible to look at that number and not think about all the druggies calling Rick for their fix. The truth was Jake's older (but not especially smarter) brother made supplemental income selling drugs. He'd been doing that since high school. Moving to the desert Southwest had inadvertently allowed him to "expand operations." Or maybe it'd been a reason for his move. Rick always acted strait-laced and managed to "fool" their parents, who always preferred to remain oblivious.

Jake had blown off the open invite at the time but kept the possibility in mind, should he need an excuse to get away and use the vacation time he'd let add up, all to help guarantee himself being made partner with his boss. As hard as Jake had worked for the guy, the potential half-ownership of a business remained a dream.

What was this thing about dreams? Rarely did Jake even think about dreams or refer to them, and he hardly remembered them as it was. However, he just had a dream that was actually a nightmare, which he'd had while taking a nap when he never usually took a nap, and . . . It was too disconcerting to even think about right now, even though he was out here walking aimlessly around the apartment complex, doing just that! Smoking was secondary, as he'd wanted to look at his Camaro "one last time for the day," but he'd already put it in the garage and parked his work truck in front of the door. His walk had taken him everywhere but on that side of the residential buildings.

To keep from lighting up a third time, Jake headed back to his apartment. If he wanted to do any more thinking about the day, it'd be necessary to do so there. No sooner did he head to the nearest entryway when none other than Mrs. Melkin appeared seemingly out of nowhere, walking her mutt, Barry.

Glancing one last time at Mrs. Melkin and her dog, Jake finally noticed the animal distinctly resembled Rags! Maybe his memory was short regarding what his childhood dog looked like, but something was still weird. Were his eyes playing tricks on him?

Jake didn't want to be obvious about avoiding waving to a neighbor, so he ducked back inside the building before the resident big-mouth Mrs. Melkin saw him. Not to portray her in a bad light, as she undoubtedly meant well, but she talked so much it was ridiculous! That drove Jake insane, and he felt like he already was.

It was time to sit down and do nothing but go over the events of the day. There had to be a chronological order somewhere, even if none appeared to exist. The problem was attempting to distinguish between a dream and reality.

Jake's launch into seemingly "another reality" began when his brother called him from Phoenix, waking him from an unprecedented afternoon nap. Jake didn't get a lot of phone calls as it was. Even though Rick hadn't contacted him by phone since right before he was about to move, given the way he opened the conversation sounded like the two brothers were close and kept in touch: "Hey Jake. It's Rick. I've gotta question for ya."

Surprised by the unexpectedness of a phone call, including the fact it was his brother, Jake had said, "Yeah?" in response to what he assumed really was a question. With his wayward brother, there was no telling.

"I just had a mind-blowingly famous celebrity stroll into my showroom and after looking over what I had there and what was in the back bein' worked on, asked if I knew any-one who had a powder blue, sixty-seven Camaro in good con-dition. Price is no object."

Meanwhile, Jake had already raised his antennae, so to speak, anticipating having his brother proceed to request the title to Jake's Camaro be Fed Exed to him, something ridiculous.

"Bro, what do you say?" Rick asked. "You up for selling your baby?"

"I have to think about it."

"Of course you do!"

Possibly the sarcasm in his brother's voice was imagined but Jake doubted it. Rather than be angry, it was imperative he keep his cool, so he calmly told Rick, "I'll call you one way or another."

"You got my cell number, right?"

"Yes, I do. Kelly wrote it. . ."

"I'll be waiting to hear from you, man," Rick declared.

There was a dial tone before Jake could say good-bye. Unlike himself, Rick never was polite and didn't mind cutting people off, not only in conversations. (He owed child support to two kids but found a way to get out of paying it.)

The beginning of this particular Saturday drive was much-anticipated, just like any other. Since Jake worked on vehicles all week, he liked nothing other than to hit the road when he had some free time (and weather was permitting). For the first few miles there was the most traffic and nothing much to see, so he typically fiddled with the radio, trying to find just the right classic rock song to match his upbeat mood. It took a good twenty minutes of driving straight south from Parker for Jake to reach the area where he finally enjoyed the driving itself (because of the scenery as well as the absence of vehicles, even on the weekend). Admittedly, he only appreciated "his favorite road" if it was driven south to north. That meant he had to take a different road south and then one west, to reach it.

Once Jake was headed north on 100E, he felt more relaxed than ever. For a few miles there was only a house here and there, each of which was in the distance. The topography consisted of small sand ridges and scruffy-looking pastures, although he had yet to see any grazing livestock. There were also clusters of oak trees as well as very tall, stately-looking pines. He had no idea what vegetation was indigenous to the area, but everything appeared surreal whenever he came here. Typically he'd turn the radio off in order to fully enjoy this part of the drive without any distractions. It was strange, how at home he felt as soon as he started driving north on 100E. (He had no idea why all north-south rural roads had an "E" or "W" after their numbers.) Anyway, it wasn't like he had a desire to actually move here, which was just as well because there was never a for sale sign in front of any property, not even for an unwanted item or vehicle. There wasn't even firewood available for purchase, although there was undoubtedly plenty of that, given all the trees surrounding the residences.

Usually Jake liked how perfect "his" road was, but on this particular day he couldn't help but see (and feel) the area for what it was: Bizarre! Nonetheless, he didn't let himself get all freaked-out by this observation. Given how lonely Jake had been ever since he and Louise broke up, he figured the feeling was a result of having been alone too long.

One strange element was the ongoing absence of a single person doing anything outside when Jake would drive past the properties. Obviously that took only a couple seconds, but given how the weather was usually pleasant and it was the weekend . . . If he ever thought like this before, he pushed the notion away. The whole area could have doubled for a movie set; all you needed were the actors!

Doing the unprecedented, Jake turned the radio on "to get through the rest of the drive." Something really didn't feel right, even though the car was cruising along perfectly. Rarely did it have a problem, not while on one of these outings.

Then there was a sudden feeling of the right rear wheel

running over something large enough to cause some damage, so he pulled over and killed the engine before getting out to investigate. If an animal was involved, he was concerned about that too.

There was a dog lying to the right of the car, just off the road, its eyes closed with tongue lolling. He sure as hell looked dead or would be, soon. Jake felt horrible about what happened, but it was the owner's fault, having let the dog run loose. The best thing to do was leave, as it appeared he was guilty of some sort of wrongdoing, yet he couldn't help feeling entirely indignant, at least for the time being.

One last glance at the dog, and Jake swore the animal resembled Rags, just like Mrs. Melkin's mutt did. However, her dog Barry always was black and white, while this one *was* originally brown but *changed* to black and white. Of course that was impossible, but then again, it had taken Jake an extra second to notice the dog lying on the sandy shoulder of the road *because the animal had been a different color and blended right in!*

Back in the car, Jake sat for a couple minutes, staring straight ahead, attempting to convince himself he imagined the dog he "accidentally killed" had fur that changed colors. After all, he didn't also imagine the dog itself, did he?

Jake was about to start his car when from the right window he noticed two boys seemingly materialize in the gravel driveway, riding bicycles. The Camaro happened to be parked about fifteen or twenty feet past the driveway, and the tan, wood-sided, A-frame house at the end of it was a good hundred yards from the road. Therefore, it was possible no one even noticed the unfortunate accident that just took place, although Jake wasn't betting on it. However, he did bet the dog was owned by the family who lived there.

As Jake attempted to remain inconspicuous, the boys (about nine and eleven) approached and were soon even with the rear end of his Camaro. Even though they were chatting, they had ample opportunity to notice "their" dead dog.

Instead, they appeared entirely oblivious and pedaled right past the car, turning right afterward. They didn't glance at his car even once!

Obviously Jake wanted nothing more than to head home, but he was hesitant to continue north on 100E because he'd have to pass the two kids. He hadn't closely seen their faces but had a feeling he would, thanks to them stopping him in the road and chewing him out for killing their dog. Making an effort to clarify matters would be entirely futile.

The craven alternative was to take "the long way home," which Jake hesitated to do out of stubbornness relative to believing something extremely creepy was going on (therefore admitting he was afraid). Nor did he want to see the kids' faces. Maybe he'd watched too many horror movies, causing his imagination to run wild at a time like this.

Jake made a quick U-turn in the road, not seeing a soul as he made his departure. Meanwhile, he made a point of not even glancing in the direction where the dog had been lying.

After driving only a couple hundred yards, Jake felt dramatically better. It had to do with physically getting away from where he'd been. Still, he was on edge and doubted he'd feel relaxed anytime soon, but his stomach managed to growl a couple times, reminding him he liked to stop in Hamlet to pick up lunch. It was about halfway between where he currently was and his place in Parker. Although Hamlet was fittingly very small, Interstate 65 ran north-south on the east side of it, and several businesses had recently sprung up at the Hamlet exit, including a couple fast-food restaurants not found near the historic downtown.

Driving in silence, it didn't even occur to Jake to turn on the radio, so he had no excuse whatsoever for "being distracted" before nearly driving over a small, white, long-haired mutt. Hitting this dog would have been "his fault," not a case of the animal running into his car. At this point he was just glad the dog didn't suddenly acquire some black spots. Then

Jake wouldn't have had any choice but to finally believe something surreal was going on.

Jake ended up skipping the stop at his favorite fast-food drive-through, having suddenly lost his appetite. He'd wanted to stop there if only to get a dose of familiarity. Given his living arrangement, the only familiar faces he saw on the weekend were the ones at the drive-through. Even though there was seemingly constant employee turn-over, whenever Jake's Camaro appeared, someone he recognized would emerge and greet him. The gesture didn't sound like much but it was to him!

Going home was obviously the next-best option, although Jake wasn't looking forward to spending the rest of the day holed up, alone. He wished nothing more than to have a dog of his own right now. It was time to seriously reconsider leaving the animal alone all day in the apartment while he was at work. If his ex-girlfriend was still employed at the humane society, he could visit her and adopt an unwanted dog. She'd most likely found someone who'd proposed if not married her. One thing (of many) she didn't like about him was his reluctance to at least buy her "a promise ring."

Another thought: if Jake actually received half-ownership of "Bart's Auto Repair," he could bring his dog to work. As long as the animal was safely out of the way . . .

That was a dumb idea! Not only that, Jake was still getting ahead of himself by taking the possibility seriously, he would ever be made the partner of a successful business.

Home again, Jake was suddenly so exhausted it felt like he'd been drugged. All he cared about was taking a nap, but he did put his car back in the garage and parked his truck back in front of the door.

The living room was what Jake's apartment entryway first led to, with the kitchen to the left and a dining area on the right. On the far side of the dining set left behind by the residents before him, was the door to his bedroom, which he couldn't reach fast enough. He almost opted for napping on the navy leather sofa he brushed past but didn't want a crick in his neck when he woke up.

Before falling asleep it occurred to Jake he might have neglected to lock the door, something he often did and was nagged about by his ex. Louise never lived with him, so he always wondered why she made such a big deal out of this oversight. Later she would start complaining about everything else "he did wrong" (including failing to give her some sort of ring), and he'd had enough. Therefore, it was actually a mutual break-up, but at this point he just wanted to see her.

That was Jake's last thought before he essentially passed out, although technically he only fell asleep. He proceeded to have a dream that began by mirroring his drive earlier in the day, but it took a dark turn when he went ahead with his usual route, versus taking a detour after a dog ran into his car. However, the animal didn't change color, not that he was aware.

After driving about a third of a mile, Jake noticed a crowd appear a couple hundred yards ahead, effectively blocking the entire road. He could have made a U-turn, but he was compelled to continue in the direction of the fray. The closer he got to the crowd, the more uneasy he became because apparently no one intended to move.

Rather than lose his cool, Jake resolved to do anything but that. Slowing his speed, he continued to approach and opened both windows all the way in order to talk to anyone who might be willing to do so and be reasonable about it. If the residents of this street had ganged up on him because they thought he'd somehow "intentionally" killed a neighborhood dog, he wanted nothing more than to make an attempt to clear his name in front of all the nearby residents.

Not surprisingly, Jake was forced to stop, as his car was swarmed by the residents of this street he once liked and had looked forward to visiting. He couldn't even claim that about

11

any people he knew, including his parents. And they lived in Parker for most of the year, only recently having discovered the state of Florida.

Just when it occurred to Jake to close the windows and attempt to back out of this unwarranted situation, who should emerge from the crowd but the same two boys he'd seen in the driveway earlier. They were walking alongside their bikes but dropped them upon seeing Jake in his beloved car. In turn, the crowd made plenty of room for them.

Finally both kids were at the driver's side window and wordlessly stared at him, but the thing was, they *had* no eyes, just empty sockets! One of them, he couldn't tell which, aggressively stuck his bare arm in the window, intending to grab Jake's neck. The arm itself had thick, patchy tufts of brown fur, while the hand was large and calloused, with dirty, yellowed, overgrown fingernails.

Then Jake woke up, his heart feeling like it was beating hard enough for him to be having a heart attack. It was possible he'd had a mild one, given all the stress he'd been feeling lately, even before this unfortunate incident involving a dog. Was it still light out? How come it seemed like he couldn't see? That was a pathetically ridiculous question, but . . . Didn't he come back inside after going for a walk, following a nap he didn't intend to take, to review the day? What the hell now? Was he awake? Why couldn't he see? Was he having a nightmare inside a nightmare, inside a . . . Or did he suddenly lose his eyesight, all because he was so stressed? Or did he lose his eyesight in a nightmare? The possibilities were endless.

Louise was terribly worried about someone she thought she didn't care about anymore, having mutually agreed to break up. Even though she'd initially been relieved to have ended her relationship with him, she came to miss his myriad quirks, habits, hang-ups . . . And she missed *him.* She had her own idiosyncrasies and needed to quit being so judgmental. Failing to establish another relationship (after many one-date failures) really made Louise change her outlook. Truthfully, not only did she miss Jake, she was ready to throw her arms around his neck and declare she loved him! Anything to let him know she still cared.

Since Jake typically didn't answer his phone even if he was home, Louise figured the best plan of action was to stop by his apartment. Never before had she dropped by unannounced, but since they were no longer even dating, what difference did it make? That sounded so breezy, but it was exactly how she felt (unafraid of being imposing). If Jake was married (which she highly doubted), Louise was happy to meet his wife as well.

Even though Louise lived in the town of Parker, as did Jake, she resided on the outskirts, which afforded some property for all the dogs she'd adopted from the humane society where she worked six days a week. She had never caught even a glimpse of him since the end of their relationship. The auto repair shop where he was employed was obviously the only place to find him during the week. So when did he run errands? On the weekend, he was either out driving his esteemed classic Camaro or hanging out in his apartment—unless he was putting in some extra time washing and waxing his coveted car.

As soon as Louise got off work at the humane society on Saturday around four-thirty, she first went home to let her dogs out and feed them a late lunch. Then she changed into "something more comfortable" for meeting a guy she hadn't seen in (how long?) awhile. Louise only wanted to make him miss her, like she was obviously missing him.

Driving to Jake's apartment, Louise was cursing herself for not making some sort of excuse for running into her ex, namely keeping her old Dodge Durango, which Jake used to service. After they broke up (and she got a pay raise), she traded it for a new one. Her mother was so glad Louise was no longer seeing Jake, she pitched in on the down-payment.

13

The last excuse her daughter needed for seeing Jake Marsh, was to visit the car repair shop where he happened to work, because her SUV broke down yet again.

Before parking and heading to Jake's second-floor apartment, Louise drove past the one-vehicle garage where he kept his 1967, powder blue Camaro. Given the time of day, his truck should have been parked in front of the garage, the Camaro safely tucked away.

That appeared to be the case, so Louise found a place to park and went to Jake's apartment. On her way she didn't see another soul, which seemed eerie for some reason.

As soon as Louise was close to his door, it flew open and there stood Jake, smiling, something he rarely did. His teeth were so shiny-white, she could hardly keep from staring at them, mesmerized. Finally, however, she looked up and saw the rest of his face—and he had no eyes, just empty sockets!

Certain she was having a nightmare, Louise rubbed her eyes as hard as she could, to make sure she woke up.

It didn't work. Or she was awake all along. All she could do was scream in pain and with dread.

Nothing Like Getting What You Want—
To Get What You Really Need

Derek was literally "up a tree" because a big, black dog ran at him in the back yard of his girlfriend's house, where they lived together. She had a dog, but it wasn't this mean thing. Since Derek wasn't a mooch, why was he not warned a mongrel was back here? It was obviously planned, having the dog roaming around back here, as the tan-colored, cinder block wall that enclosed the yard was too tall for an animal to scale—except maybe one of the wild boars that roamed around here from time to time, in Scottsdale, Arizona. Couldn't they jump high?

Admittedly Derek knew little about all animals and happened to hate dogs. Granted, it was a pre-conceived notion about them and was perhaps unfair. His opinion could still be changed, and if any dog could do that, it was Timmy, his girlfriend's dog. The mutt was rescued from the pound and clearly "loved" Eva but always steered clear of Derek. Hey, the feeling was mutual—and that helped make things go in the wrong direction when Derek unexpectedly got off work early.

Ever step in a fresh pile of dog poop *and* you hate dogs? Not the best combination. To think, Derek stepped in the pile (barefoot) shortly before realizing perhaps Timmy wasn't so bad after all and deserved some consideration. But Derek was getting ahead of himself with his story.

By the way, Derek was not afraid of dogs – except this "thing" that had scared the hell out of him. Why else would Derek be crouched on the limb of a lemon tree, about six feet

15

off the ground? Apparently fruit trees have pretty strong limbs, not that he was a big guy or fat. As much as he hated to exercise, other than "shooting hoops," he liked to think he looked good. Of course it was easier to brag about as much at 32 than twenty years from now. Anyway, he *tried* to take walks with "Eva and Timmy," but he got the distinct impression he wasn't really welcome. She walked him three or four times a day and no longer visited the dog park.

After having lived with Eva for six months (following dating her for close to two months), it was revealed she'd been taking Timmy to the dog park not for him but for her: She'd been hoping to meet "a fellow dog lover"; fall madly in love with him; and live happily ever after with him and their dogs. Since Camelback Park was within easy walking distance of Eva's house, it was in fact the perfect destination for her matchmaking pursuit. Unfortunately she wasn't having any luck, and it was thanks to Derek, her dream was "sort of able to come true."

On the fateful New Year's Day Derek first laid eyes on Eva, she was in "the dog park portion" of Camelback Park, half-heartedly throwing a light blue rubber ball to her big-looking, long-legged, black and tan-colored pooch. That was his observation, anyway. (Later Derek would find out Timmy was a Labrador/German shepherd mix.) It had been impossible not to take notice of the only other park patron, and he also didn't fail to notice there were no vehicles, aside from his white Mitsubishi Eclipse, parked alongside 62nd Street, where the park was located. Therefore, "she" (and her dog) lived in the neighborhood. Most of the houses were older, modest, ranch-style, no more than a couple thousand square feet, but some of the larger lots had "re-builds" on them, and each new house was huge and imposing-looking, taking up most of the lot.

Proudly holding his basketball, about to spend an hour or two "shooting hoops," Derek almost said, "Happy New Year!" just for the hell of it, but "the lady with the dog" would have thought it was directed at her. (Perhaps sub-con-sciously it would have been.)

Derek kept his mouth shut and instead really looked at her. Granted, she wasn't very close, but from what he could see (and he had 20/20 vision—no glasses or contacts), she was positively gorgeous, even bundled up in a long-sleeved, gray hoodie and matching sweatpants. Simultaneously he forgot she had a dog, making her "a dog person." Women always had a way of making Derek fail to think logically. In this situation, it didn't help he not only hadn't been in a seri-ous relationship for close to a year (he hadn't gotten laid), he felt something super-intense about this female. O.K., the truth: he was OBSESSED with her. There was something about her letting that long, brown hair hang loose while busy with her dog . . . It was a version of "multi-tasking" and drove him insane with desire.

Bundled up like she was, possibly the "winter weather" was actually cold for her. That meant she was either a native of the area or was from southern California. Derek was orig-inally from the Midwest and only had on navy cotton shorts and a red, short-sleeved cotton T-shirt. It was maybe 45 degrees Fahrenheit this morning, a welcomed respite from the summer heat. As it was, he never failed to sweat a lot once he got into "shooting hoops."

Barely did Derek settle into his favorite form of exercise when he heard "her" say, "Come on, Timmy. Let's go home." He whirled around to see her putting a leash on her pooch. Just like that! She *could not* simply leave; he was obsessed with her!

Since she (and her dog) obviously lived within walking distance of the park, Derek decided to shamelessly watch where they headed. If they disappeared from view before reaching home, he'd jump in his car and follow them. In the meantime he'd play basketball.

Almost out of sight, the two made a left turn into a drive-way at the far southeast side of 62nd Street. Derek stood transfixed, memorizing exactly which concrete driveway was the one leading to "her" house. Then again, what made him think she lived there with just her dog? Only Derek could stand to live alone for any length of time, and his rental didn't allow pets, so he couldn't have owned a dog if he wanted to. As it was, the lease was expiring in a couple months, and he was ready to move. For what he paid in rent, there were few amenities, although his place was certainly above average.

Derek finally started shooting hoops with his full attention and got plenty of exercise, as he was excited yet concerned whether he'd see this woman again. Somehow he had to find out if she was married, so for starters he would drive past "her" house later in the day and hopefully find an indication she was married or "taken" in whatever capacity. At the rate he was exerting himself, he'd need a nap when he got home, which would help kill time.

The beginning of things "not going as usual" (and then *really* veering off the tracks), was when Derek's boss showed up at the store about 4:30 and ordered him to leave early. Derek had never questioned anything his boss told him to do, so he followed Mr. Tan's order. All that mattered was he hadn't been fired.

Fortunately Derek had had the wherewithal to close the sliding glass door when he'd originally come out to the back yard to check on what had Timmy too agitated to "go out and do his thing." Eva always bragged about how well-housebroken her dog was, yet while she and Derek were at their respective jobs, she made sure the animal was confined to the kitchen/utility room, which also had a 3/4th bathroom. Derek never dared chide his girlfriend about her level of trust regarding her pooch. Besides, that was the only part of the house that had a tile floor, and she'd recently replaced the carpet in a couple other rooms.

Suddenly more infuriated than ever with "his predicament," Derek decided to descend this tree and return to the "safety" of the house. From what little peripheral vision he had up here (the dense amount of leaves practically blocked his view, even straight ahead), it *appeared* "the monster-dog" was nowhere to be seen.

Just as Derek was about to put his left (bare) foot on the ground, he felt a tug on his favorite khaki pants. For a split second he thought it was all in his imagination. Then he lifted his leg and found it took some effort—*and something ripped his pants* as he re-ascended the lemon tree.

"Shit!" he yelled after managing to get enough of a toe-hold to take a look at the hack-job this #@!% mutt just did on his favorite khakis. He was lucky his foot wasn't mangled too! Who knew if the thing had its rabies shot, although Eva had mentioned Maricopa County was exceptionally stringent about requiring dog owners to prove their charges received regular rabies vaccinations.

Did he have a puncture wound *anywhere?* Derek wondered. If this monster-dog possibly wasn't recently given the rabies vaccination, he could sue—if he lived long enough. The problem was he couldn't get a good look at his legs and feet while crouched on a lemon tree branch!

Derek managed to come to his senses somewhat—what was left of them—and glared at the big, long-haired, coal black dog that was sitting there, obviously proud of itself. Sickening. Then Derek looked in the direction of the house, where Timmy sat erect at the sliding glass door. Derek never imagined his heart going out to a dog, but it did to Timmy at that moment, thanks to how the animal had "indirectly" tried to warn Derek it was unsafe to go in the back yard. Meanwhile, Derek had been too angry to take stock of the situation. All in all, he was relieved to discover some merit in Timmy. Obviously the dog wasn't a dolt—unlike what Derek felt he himself was, especially when stranded in a lemon tree. Embarrassingly, Derek had made a point of avoiding Timmy ever since moving in with the dog's owner, six months ago.

Once Eva got home from work, this nightmare would end. She had to know whose deranged dog this was, roaming around in her back yard. Would Derek expect some sort of apology from her? No! What would end up happening was *he* would apologize to *her* for "upsetting the visiting dog," some such nonsense. Eva ruled the roost, no doubt about it, but it was her house. As much as he loved her (but was afraid to say the "L-word" because men *never* said it first— right?), Derek wondered what was in store for them as a couple because at some point this fact *would* matter: they had nothing in common.

Glancing over at the sliding glass door again, Derek noticed Timmy was no longer there. What the hell *was* the dog doing? Taking another shit on the kitchen floor? That "habit" of the dog's, was how Derek ended up being barefoot!

It was time to go back to when Derek came home from work early and answered his phone for the seemingly innocuous fact Eva had been calling him. He happened to be just inside the kitchen, having entered via the garage. He parked his car there, per Eva's insistence, as she preferred to use the carport for her new Mazda 3. He never questioned her logic; he simply did as he was told. So that was how he ended up listening to these instructions, once he made the mistake of telling her he was home early from work: "Great! You can feed Timmy and let him out. You know where I keep his food and the bowl, in the corner."

After a good-bye, see you soon, Eva hung up and that was that. Derek had wanted to remind her, "her dog and her boyfriend" had purposely avoided one another the entire six months they'd been living under the same roof.

The call finished, naturally Derek couldn't wait to be finished altogether with the damned phone, so he turned it off and left it on the kitchen counter, right by the door leading to the garage. He didn't even bother to charge it!

It wasn't unheard of for Derek to remove his shoes as

soon as he returned home from work, although he typically was wearing socks. On this particular day, he had left the house wearing a pair of canvas slip-ons he'd recently purchased and didn't think he needed socks with them. What a mistake that was. (He was only trying to find a way to eliminate some laundry, since he was responsible for his own.) So once he was in the door, he couldn't wait to remove his shoes, which Eva preferred he do, anyway.

Initially Derek didn't even see Timmy, which should have been impossible, given the limited area the dog was contained in as well as the fact the animal weighed at least fifty pounds.

Then Timmy was located, "hiding" behind the kitchen table and chairs, which was to the right of the sliding glass door. The dog couldn't seem to decide if he was more interested in looking outside or keeping an eye on Derek.

"Hey, Timmy," Derek said. "It's you and me for a little bit, 'til your mistress comes home. I'm gonna get your lunch ready, in case you want to eat before you go outside, but you seem like you might want to go out right now. Maybe we should just plan on that. I gotta agree, you've got a pretty nice back yard to roam around in." The concrete patio was larger than the original, smallish square because formerly there was an in-ground pool that had been concreted-over. Beyond the concrete area there was plenty of grass for Timmy to enjoy himself. For shade there were two tall, leafy, thick-trunked lemon trees.

Derek went to the sliding glass door and opened it for Timmy, expecting the dog to go outside. Instead the dog scuttled to the other side of the kitchen table and huddled by none other than the door leading to the garage! Clearly Timmy had some sort of issue with Derek; at the same time, Derek was in no position to complain, given his feelings toward Timmy!

Nonetheless, Derek owed it to Eva (and their relationship), to make sure Timmy went out and had lunch, despite how difficult that was proving to accomplish. And at this point it was a matter of making the dog go out no matter what. *Then* lunch. Otherwise, there would be "repercussions," for sure.

No sooner did Derek almost get a hold of Timmy's brown leather collar (it took a lot of nerve for Derek to even try to grab it), and the furry "little" shit took off, going back behind the kitchen table, even though the sliding glass door was wide open!

Furious, Derek went in hot pursuit of Timmy, and just as he was about to grab the dog's collar yet again, the animal shied away, causing Derek to nearly fall on his face. After taking a couple quick steps forward to maintain his balance, Derek felt something gooey and warm squishing between the toes of his left (bare) foot. Not only that, it smelled!

"I stepped in dog shit!" Derek yelled, hardly able to look or he'd throw up for sure. Meanwhile he spied Timmy, who was back by the door leading to the garage. "Thanks, you shit!" he exclaimed and slammed shut the sliding glass door. Then he hopped over to the shower in the 3/4th bathroom, grateful for the fact it was here. Its original purpose was most likely a place for swimmers to shower off before or after going in the pool—back when it existed.

Derek managed to keep from leaving dog shit everywhere on his way to the bathroom, but there was still the pile itself to deal with, which he'd do after Timmy was finally outside. Hopefully in the meantime Eva would return home and could take care of it. She could also spare Derek from having to take care of a dog who hated him. At the same time, Derek realized he did not hate Timmy after all; it was a matter of finally having given the dog a chance by looking at things from Timmy's perspective. It was an amazing transition for a "dog-hater"—or former dog-hater (?).

There was no explanation as to why Derek had been determined to shut the sliding glass door before washing off his foot (and getting his left pants leg wet). With the dog shit removed, he quickly left the bathroom and opened the sliding glass door again. This time he went outside and called Timmy from the patio, attempting to sound "calm and sweet," just like Eva never failed to do, even if she was furious with her dog, which she was on occasion. She also stood outside to call him, although that never happened because Timmy otherwise refused to go out (that Derek was aware).

Not surprisingly, Timmy was unresponsive to the point he didn't even bother to appear at the doorway. At the same time, Derek didn't let as much get to him. Thanks to this %@#! dog, Derek was learning a lot about himself and was grateful for that alone. Whatever else he gained from the situation, was a bonus.

After calling Timmy's name one last time (what the hell), Derek heard a rumbling behind him and initially didn't know what to think. So what did he "logically" do but close the sliding glass door and sprint for the closest lemon tree, barely glancing at whatever was on his heels the approximate thirty-foot distance between the tree trunk and where he'd been standing.

Crouching on the lowest branch, Derek had an opportunity to look at his adversary, which was none other than a big, long-legged, black-haired dog with a boxy head and dark, mean-looking eyes. Since this shit just "treed" Derek, it was impossible to describe the dog as "nice and furry."

Still, there was no reasonable explanation as to why Derek would climb this lemon tree, versus just jump back in the house and close the damned door, other than the fact he was compelled to keep avoiding Timmy and his poop. And for someone who wasn't even remotely a dog person . . . Besides, Derek was practically addicted to climbing trees when he was eight to about twelve-years-old. Living in a desert climate, the tree-climbing choices were limited, especially where (and how) he grew up.

The worst part was being in a lemon tree at age thirty-two, in his girlfriend's back yard, but not because he wanted to. Obviously this was what he got for being obsessed with a female who loved dogs and let another "dog lover" leave her dog here. He assumed it was a woman who owned this piece of s—t. There. He tried to show some respect for the mongrel and its idiot owner but honestly couldn't.

All Derek asked was the stupid dog quit sitting by the tree, staring up at him. It only added to Derek's humiliation. Plus, it wasn't easy crouching here, although he could sort of stand, to keep from getting stiff. His devotion to "shooting hoops" came in handy, or he wouldn't have had the stamina for this unexpected situation.

Regarding Timmy, he'd FINALLY made his way to the sliding glass door, most likely having just caught some of the proceedings. Now that things died back down, where the hell was Eva? Even though he didn't have his phone he had his watch, and it was almost 5:30. If she needed to run errands after work, she never failed to tell him. Then again, the fact Derek hadn't been warned about this box-headed monster having taken up residence in the back yard, even temporarily, went hand-in hand with the rest of Eva's failure to communicate openly with him.

Derek heard a car door slam, and it sounded like it came from under the carport. So that meant Eva had to be home, which was such a relief he actually started to cry! Surely everything would be explained shortly. And later Derek vowed to offer to take Timmy for a walk, just the two of them. Eva would be pleasantly surprised (he hoped). However, he wouldn't make the offer just to please her; he sincerely wanted to spend some one-on-one time with Eva's dog. This "experience" involving someone's mutt had changed Derek's mindset.

Standing straight (or as straight as possible), Derek's knees hurt like hell for a few seconds. It was what he got for not shooting hoops for a few days. Long ago (in his teens and early twenties), he was into distance running and only quit because his knees were in so much pain. Maybe he could try some around-the-block jogging, should he want another form of exercise.

The mutt suddenly turned and loped over to the gate that opened to the carport and front yard. Phew! Derek could go in the house and greet Eva, salvaging the day yet. So he began descending the tree and had just put his left foot on the ground when the sliding glass door was opened, and Eva was heard talking to a person—versus Timmy. Then he heard a woman laugh, so Derek went back up the tree, hoping to "hide" until "they" left. This was ridiculous! But he went through with the plan anyway, not sure why he didn't just confront them both, other than the possibility he was embarrassed?

After a moment's contemplation Derek realized he was indeed embarrassed—for them! And he was willing to bet "the other woman" was none other than the owner of the mongrel that had been harassing him. Then Eva stepped outside, with none other than Georgia Palmer "on her heels." The damned bitch literally looked like a poodle with that huge poof of corkscrew-curly, light blonde hair. It was kept out of her eyes by her sunglasses, perched atop her head. Derek was guarded about her before, but now he absolutely hated her, even more than he hated her dog. But thanks to Timmy, Derek no longer hated dogs in general, and his feelings were actually more positive than just that.

Supposedly Georgia's husband gave her that dog because the guy traveled a lot for his job, and she didn't like being left home, alone. Nonetheless it was her responsibility, how the thing acted. The good news was they didn't have any kids—yet.

It wasn't lost on Derek, how Eva made sure to shut the sliding glass door once Georgia and she were on the patio. Also, Timmy was still nowhere in sight. While both women looked around, Derek expected to be found out. Instead they remained oblivious to his presence, and Georgia, only concerned with her block-headed pooch, asked, "Where's Titan?"

Derek had to roll his eyes upon hearing that name. Obviously it fit in someone's mind's eye, if only the damned dog's!

Then stupid Titan appeared from around the corner, wagging its tail and actually appearing to smile (versus snarling). Derek had never paid any attention to something like that, but he sure as hell was learning fast.

"Hey, Titan, my little lover-boy," Georgia said and kissed the dog on the mouth. Ugh! Eva didn't do that with Timmy (that Derek was aware). Since no one had mentioned anything about the pile of dog crap on the kitchen floor, it was anyone's guess if either one had even noticed it. After cooing over her a-hole of a dog for a good half-minute, Georgia told Eva, "Thanks for letting me leave my baby here for the day. Like I mentioned, he was getting along great with the painters, until one was bitten. I'd repeatedly reassured them Titan would leave them alone in the back yard, as long as they ignored him. So one guy must have run at him with a paint roller, for the heck of it. That's all I can figure."

Meanwhile, Derek furiously shook his head, hardly able to believe Georgia was entirely clueless about her own dog! The damned thing had some serious issues. Then again, given how clueless Georgia was, overall. . . She then asked Eva, "Where's Derek? Didn't you mention he got off work early?"

"Yeah, he did," Eva replied, suddenly looking around (but never "up," even a little). Duh! Obviously it never occurred to her to warn him about Titan, yet suddenly none of this was surprising. She added, "He must be at the park, 'shooting hoops,' as he calls it. Basically it consists of him playing basketball with himself." After exchanging a look with Georgia, both women burst into laughter. Titan sat beside his owner and smiled.

It took everything in Derek's power not to scream, "You bitches!" Throw in idiotic Titan, too. If only the dog had any idea what it would have inferred!

That was enough to compel Derek to laugh, but he managed to hold it in. He'd wait for all three of them to get out of the way, and he was out of here. It wasn't like he didn't have enough money to find a place to live while locating a new, "permanent" place. (Renting was still his most favorable option.) But it had to allow dogs, because he intended to adopt one. And he only had to be agile enough to accompany Derek on a slow jog every day, probably in the morning, unless "they" decided to sleep late. So Derek was leaving a woman he'd been obsessed with but with whom he had nothing in common. Ironically he did, however, thanks to her (and her dog).

Amy Kristoff

Tucker: The Hero for Many Reasons

"Mommy, I want to be just like you when I grow up," Gina said to her mother, Sonia, as the latter tucked her daughter into bed about 8:30, the evening of the first day of first grade at Arcadia Elementary School in Scottsdale, Arizona. That meant it had been a full day of school, and although Gina appeared to be O.K. with as much, Sonia was sick about her. Nonetheless, she kissed her daughter on the forehead and told her good night, she loved her, before leaving her room, shutting the door. That was essentially Sonia's answer to what her daughter said. In other words, Sonia ignored her! At six-years-old, Gina was way too young to comprehend why her mother didn't consider herself a role model, albeit not because she was immoral, nothing like that. It was a matter of being a doormat to everyone, particularly her estranged husband, Michael. And he'd abruptly left because he was "bored." No further explanation was required of him, thanks to how easily Sonia accepted what he told her. Given the fact they'd been married almost ten years before he left, even she thought a more detailed explanation was in order. However, she was "too polite" to make a request for as much, not that he would have provided it. He'd already moved in with his new girlfriend, which said it all, as far as what he was after: someone new to screw! That sounded crass but was the truth. Michael was a self-made financial success (but had start-up help from his wealthy parents), while Sonia came from practically nothing and still would have been scraping by, if she hadn't caught her future husband's eye.

28

DOGS AND THEIR TWISTED TALES

Even before Gina started first grade, she'd been showing a bit of an attitude, but it wasn't like she'd gotten smart-alecky with Sonia, nothing like that. Maybe it was just a matter of her daughter having become very defensive once her father left home (and she knew why, if only in vague terms). Sonia didn't bother to gloss over this situation because it was so hurtful, everyone deserved to feel the pain. That sounded awful but was how Sonia felt at the time—and still did. That said, she tried to make light of the whole predicament. "The other woman" had even met Gina, as Michael had brought her to the house "to visit" for a few minutes a couple weekends ago. What Sonia found the most disturbing was the way Annette ("the other woman") kept looking at Gina. If Sonia did say so herself, the woman was no more physically attractive than herself, although she was probably a few years younger and had long black hair, which she kept loose. Meanwhile, Sonia had light brown hair that was shoulder length but spent most of its time in a ponytail. Fortunately Sonia was taller than her by at least a couple inches, thanks to her long legs. Nonetheless, since Annette was a fitness instructor (and never had kids) she was admittedly the more fit-looking one.

If it sounded like Sonia had been sizing up her competition, it was true. And she wasn't at all ashamed about as much; it was frustrating she failed to pay more attention to Annette and how she acted, other than eerily being "very interested" in Gina. Granted, Gina was very cute and sweet, but she was no pushover, even at her tender age. (It was at times maddening to observe as much, given what a wallflower Sonia was at her daughter's age.)

Ever since Michael abruptly left, Gina had been having nightmares. Her bedroom was upstairs, the first door on the left. Meanwhile, the master bedroom suite was downstairs, albeit near the staircase. Nonetheless, Sonia didn't feel as if it would ever be possible to reach her daughter quickly enough when she needed some post-nightmare consoling.

Sonia had actually considered sleeping in the spare bedroom opposite to Gina's, but if Gina became accustomed to that arrangement . . . At this point Sonia remained hopelessly optimistic Michael would come to his senses and come home. Was it even in her place to expect as much from her husband? (Low self-esteem skewed her expectations.)

Once downstairs, Sonia couldn't recall if she unintentionally locked Gina's bedroom door. A few nights ago she did just that, and Gina was upstairs wailing around midnight when Sonia hurried to reach her, only to be stopped short. Naturally there was no key for the door—or maybe there should have been. Anyway, Sonia ended up pounding on the door to make Gina open it, which she eventually did, teary-eyed and upset. Sonia was furious with herself for having neglected to make sure she didn't accidentally lock her daughter's bedroom door.

What Sonia needed to mention was she'd started a ritual ever since Michael left: she took their dog, Tucker, for a "quick walk" right after Gina was in bed. Gina never had a nightmare until later in the evening, so it seemed like "a safe activity"—and it helped Sonia de-stress. Having never been a dog person, it was amazing how easily she became one. And that was even before Michael made his sudden departure from family life. There was something about not having him home at night that made her extremely restless. Maybe she just felt like she needed to go out too, if only to walk Tucker. She usually only walked him early in the morning before anyone was out of bed or sometimes in the late afternoon. Occasionally Gina came along if she was around and wanted to accompany them.

As much as Gina liked Tucker, she was still too young (and small) to appreciate what a great companion he was. At sixty pounds, he probably weighed about the same as she did. Although he didn't "play with her," it was only because Gina was slightly intimidated by him. Given her age, that was completely understandable. Hopefully at some point she'd appreciate the reliable companionship of a dog (versus a husband).

If Gina never gave a whit about dogs or any other pet, it would certainly prove she'd inherited the disinclination from her father, who only cared about himself. As it was, Tucker was turning out to be "Sonia's dog," if only because they spent so much time together.

After Sonia went back upstairs and confirmed she'd indeed left Gina's bedroom door unlocked, she simultaneously realized she'd already confirmed as much the first time around (but forgot because she was so distracted by everything lately). While Michael remained oblivious to the havoc he'd wrought on his family, Sonia was forced to deal with it, "the why" behind taking Tucker on an evening walk. That was how she justified leaving Gina alone in the house for a few minutes. It wasn't her fault Michael was too cheap to install a security system. The number one reason Sonia was allowed to have a dog in the first place was because she kept complaining to him about how alone she felt when he was at work all day and often stayed late. Given Michael's new living arrangement with a fitness instructor he'd met at the health club (near his office), it was possible he'd never put in any overtime. It was only natural to think like that. Nonetheless, Sonia would still take him back! Maybe she was being unrealistic, which was entirely possible. Due to all this emotional mayhem, she wasn't sure how or what to think. Perhaps she ought to be relieved he'd left. Since he had yet to file any divorce papers, it could only mean it had something to do with the ten-year mark of their marriage. Thanks to some stupid paper he'd essentially told her to sign before they married (and she obediently did so, never reading it), it was a safe bet they had to stay together a decade or else he had to pay her a huge sum, particularly if he was "at fault." Clearly he was! Again, through it all, Sonia loved him so much, she'd still take him back, despite his selfish, greedy motive for not filing for divorce, as well as their "trial" separation, which was involuntary on her part.

Back downstairs, Sonia was greeted by none other than Tucker, whose bed was just around the corner of the staircase, in the wood-floor sunroom. Formerly it was where the family would sit in the evening, watching television. Ever since Michael left, Gina stayed in her room all evening, watching her own TV. Now Sonia was sorry she caved and let their daughter have a television set. It was that or a cell phone, which seemed ridiculous. As it was, Sonia felt like Gina was compelled to blame her for the fact Michael suddenly no longer lived at home. It was probably a common reaction for young children of broken homes (especially girls), but Sonia nonetheless took it extremely personally.

"Ready for your walk?" Sonia asked Tucker, pausing to pat his head before continuing to the utility room, to grab his leash. Once Gina was in bed, it felt like a timer was running in Sonia's head. Meanwhile, Tucker was already accustomed to "the new evening schedule" and loved it.

The neighborhood was conducive to walking a dog, not only because all the streets were straight and level but because of the myriad options: it was possible to take a short or long "around-the-block walk," thanks to how the streets criss-crossed. It sounded predictable, but there was always something new to see. However, there was no preparing Sonia for having verified where her husband was shacking up! Not only that, he almost backed his Lexus sedan into Tucker and herself as they were passing the residence. His look of surprise and embarrassment was almost amusing. If Michael had dared take some walks with her (and Tucker), he might have first seen his future girlfriend at home, instead. There, she probably didn't look as sexy as she did when working at the health club. Annette had been granted the house in the divorce settlement, so unless she also received a large cash settlement, she undoubtedly welcomed his company. After all, given how *generous* Michael could be (when he felt like it), there was no way he wasn't also generously helping with her monthly expenses.

Michael was going to get what he deserved because even if he filed for divorce (and only then would Sonia do the same), he'd still not only have to continue taking care of her and Gina, he'd be more legally obligated than ever to do so. Having recklessly taken up with a "dimbo" (a dumb bimbo, Sonia's own description), evidently he wasn't thinking straight. One thing Sonia had initially liked about Michael was his intelligence, as she was always drawn to that in people, not just a potential mate. Combined with his handsomeness and easy smile, what was there not to like?

Even though Sonia hadn't been living in luxury before Michael "swept her off her feet," she'd been satisfied overall with her living arrangement. In the meantime, he'd spoiled her, and she didn't want to return to her comparatively more modest lifestyle, especially with a daughter to raise. There was absolutely no reason to force innocent Gina to live any differently than she currently was. It wasn't particularly extravagant, but it was definitely secure . . . wasn't it? Why did that doubt even occur? Because life revolved around doubt and overcoming as much?

This was all too much for Sonia to sort out, so she'd walk Tucker and clear her head, try not to think about anything. The weather was beautiful, as it had been for a couple days; usually in September it was still hellishly hot.

After walking Tucker a couple minutes, Sonia felt no better. In fact, she actually felt more agitated than ever. They'd walked quite far, passing houses that were mostly ranch-style with bland-colored stucco siding and peaked roofs with asphalt shingles—not exactly a completely Southwestern look. But that was part of the area's allure; there were also plenty of houses that totally fit the description of "Southwest-style" on streets other than Vista Bonita. They had flat roofs and adobe-style or Mediterranean designs with wrought-iron accents, including window grates . . . There were also desert-scape front yards, which had stone or gravel and desert vegetation instead of grass. The desert landscape was often in front of a traditional ranch-style house, while the adobe-style one had a grass yard.

Most importantly the neighborhood was as peaceful as usual, yet Sonia found as much agitating! Also, every house and yard looked perfect, not unlike "her" home. At the same time, Sonia's personal life was a shambles. It was hypocritical, and she couldn't help wondering how many other residents were living the same lie.

That did it. Sonia turned around, abruptly pulling on Tucker's leash. Fortunately he was quick to obey because his owner was so distracted she appeared to have no patience. Sonia had planned to walk to the next corner, making a rather long, around-the-block walk, about halfway or more to where Michael lived. She felt the extra time was needed, to think.

Sonia was so sorry for having unnecessarily yanked on Tucker's leash she said, "Let's go home!" knowing that would excite him and he'd forget about her oversight.

Sure enough, Tucker immediately forgot Sonia had been abrupt with him and started pulling on the leash. Usually that annoyed her, but this evening she was tempted to start jogging to keep up with him. Despite her anxiety, it was impossible not to smile briefly.

It was funny how Michael did all the initial "pulling" in regard to introducing himself to Sonia and accomplishing much more than that. Before they'd met, she'd been minding her own business, working as a drink waitress at members-only La Colina Country Club, in Carefree. On the Saturday afternoon Michael stopped in there with his attorney-friend member, Tony Silver, Sonia was subbing for a co-worker whose son had a medical emergency. Otherwise she wouldn't have been at work until five.

Mr. Silver and his wife, Carmen, were both enjoyable to wait on and generous tippers. They were also attractive, classy, and polite; with those compliments, it would be difficult not to like anyone who joined Mr. Silver for a Saturday afternoon lunch on the terrace overlooking the pool area. Sonia would later find out the two men didn't sit on the terrace overlooking the golf course because Michael not only wasn't a golfer, he *hated* anything to do with the game.

Not to change the subject, but Michael was clearly determined to leave her for someone else. She wasn't surprised he ended up with a fitness instructor because he looked up to women who exercised (except his wife). Sonia's natural inclination to trust was essentially the problem; not only that, she'd overestimated herself. Michael had made her feel even less confident than she was when employed by La Colina Country Club. But that lack of confidence had to do with her personal life. After all, weren't you supposed to feel better about yourself after getting married (for women at least)?

The men had time to peruse the menu, and since it was lunchtime, Sonia didn't have to take a drink order prior to the lunch order; she was permitted to do both at once. So she was able to ask, "Have you two decided?" instead of: "Can I get you two a drink from the bar?"

It was outright shocking to have Mr. Silver's guest/friend reply, "Would you be available to meet someplace for dinner tonight? I'd love nothing more than to have you sitting with me at a table, rather than standing beside it, taking my order."

As flattered as Sonia was to even be noticed by "this man" (and she wasn't even in her skimpier cocktail waitress uniform), it was impossible to answer yes or no, so she ignored him. All that concerned her was potentially breaking any rules regarding "flirting with a member or guest." Meanwhile, his easy confidence was driving her insane (in a good way).

Mr. Silver had initially appeared shocked by his friend's outburst and continued to remain incredulous. Nonetheless, he attempted to appear as if everything was O.K. and ordered a Caesar salad and a diet Sprite.

Sonia was back to Mr. Silver's friend. Her heart wildly beating, she looked right into the man's piercing brown eyes and calmly repeated her question.

Tucker kept pulling on his leash to the point Sonia almost gave in and started jogging, despite wearing loafers without socks. The shoes were stretched out, causing them to easily fall off. Of all the times to realize how ill-fitting they really were! Not to give Tucker too much credit, but it appeared he was in a hurry due to something other than an intense desire to please.

"To have a companion" was the most important reason Sonia ended up with Tucker, as she'd complained to Michael about his ongoing absences, due to his devotion to work, including having to travel occasionally. At the same time, she was aware his small business financial advisory company was what enabled her to be a stay-at-home mom. As it was, Sonia had been worried about "losing her daughter all day, thanks to first grade," long before Gina actually started school again for the year. It was bad enough when she was gone half a day for kindergarten.

Meanwhile, Sonia's mother-in law (Michael's mother), Kay, had been providing a foster home for Tucker, a year-old, Doberman-Labrador cross. When Sonia "met him," she immediately felt a connection, even though she'd never before owned a dog (or any other pet). Thanks to Kay's encouragement, Sonia proceeded with the adoption.

In short order, Sonia liked to think she became a dog person. Gina enjoyed Tucker's company as well, but she was still too young to really appreciate him. Fortunately, however, he was patient with her, even protective in a way. Michael was relieved Sonia had her companionship in the form of a dog, and his mother was able to help. Conversely, it irritated him that his mother was still close to Sonia when he'd moved on to someone else. As for Kay, she had been a literal shoulder to cry on for Sonia at a time like this. And Sonia had no close family to rely on; her parents lived in northern Oregon and practically disowned her for leaving home to attend college in the desert Southwest. She didn't end up getting any sort of degree but was determined to strike out on her own. The climate in Scottsdale was the perfect antidote for her tendency to be anxious and depressed. Even though her parents would never admit it, perhaps they *didn't* always know better, especially in regard to their daughter's well-being.

Tucker pulled on the leash with even more urgency once Sonia and he were within sight of the house. By the time they were near the front stoop, she let him extend the leash as much as possible. Nonetheless, he still had to wait for her to unlock the door, which she proceeded to do, only to find it wasn't locked! Sonia very simply never would have neglected to lock the door, especially not when Gina was alone in the house.

Filled with trepidation, Sonia entered the house, Tucker right beside her but eager to resume taking the lead. She finally let him do so, and just as he started up the staircase, Gina started screaming, sounding like she was being murdered! Sonia's whole body initially felt paralyzed with apprehension before she regained her bearings and followed Tucker upstairs, every emotion going through her.

Gina's bedroom door was immediately to the left at the top of the stairs, and Tucker pushed the door open just as Sonia was almost finished ascending the staircase. Meanwhile, Gina was screaming as loudly as ever, which Sonia took as a "positive" sign.

Even before Sonia entered the bedroom, Gina's screaming was replaced by the shrieks of most likely a woman. Sonia was so stressed and upset, it would have been easy to join in; however, she vowed to keep her cool, reminding herself she'd never been guilty of histrionics. Granted, her

37

daughter had never been in jeopardy before, but it was still no time to panic. Gina needed her mother more than ever.

It was possible Sonia didn't imagine literally roaring when she barged into Gina's room and proceeded to charge at none other than Annette, Michael's girlfriend! Meanwhile, Tucker had her backed against the wall, between two narrow, whitewashed dressers. He was snarling at her, fur raised. Even if she was a dog person, Tucker's aggression would have been unnerving for her.

After Sonia finally took re-possession of Tucker's leash and pulled him away from Annette, Sonia was rewarded with being told: "It almost bit me! Keep it away!"

As if showing what he thought of that order, Tucker proceeded to lunge at Annette, but Sonia was able to restrain him a second time. Only then was she finally able to ask Annette, "Why are you in my daughter's room, let alone even in *my* house? I doubt Michael gave the O.K. and handed over the key. You would have had to steal it from him. Haven't you done enough to ruin our family? What more do you want?"

Finished speaking, Sonia became aware of the fact she was visibly shaking. Her stress-level was so high she'd completely forgotten Gina was behind her in bed.

Sure enough, Gina was there, "observing the proceedings," her arms tightly wrapped around her knees. She looked more surprised than terrified, making Sonia very proud of her.

With Tucker still on a short leash, Sonia went up to Gina and hugged her the best she could. Then Gina started crying and wanted to hug her again, so Sonia kneeled beside the bed, on her daughter's right, facing away from where Annette had been standing. Sonia kept holding Tucker's leash, but she was forced to give him some slack so she could hug her daughter again.

Suddenly Sonia realized Tucker's leash was no longer in her hand! It never occurred to her he wasn't about to give up on "the trespasser." Was Annette a potential kidnapper? Hadn't she done enough damage by seducing Sonia's husband?

Then Sonia turned around and not surprisingly Annette wasn't there. As concerned as Sonia was about Tucker—should he actually pursue Annette to the point he got outside —she was not about to leave an obviously traumatized Gina, poor thing. Tucker knew better than to just run off, so it came down to a matter of trusting him, something Sonia couldn't even do with her husband!

Gina obviously took notice of Tucker's departure, as she said, "Is Tucker coming back? Why don't you go look for him? That lady looked like Dad's girlfriend, but she was spooky this time. Why didn't she ever say anything?"

At first Sonia didn't know what to say; she wanted some answers too, at this point. That said, her daughter was owed some sort of response, so Sonia carefully replied, "Honey, I'm counting on Tucker not to leave, especially not with or on the heels of that woman, who *was* your father's girlfriend."

Gina nodded, appearing resigned. She'd returned to clasping her arms around her legs. Sonia wanted nothing more than to confess she was worried sick about Tucker; not only that she refused to leave Gina alone again.

Not two seconds later, who appeared in the doorway but Tucker, his leash taut because Michael couldn't keep up. It didn't help he was using his other hand to keep a tight hold on Annette, who was reluctantly bringing up the rear.

The first words out of Michael's mouth were, "Sonia, Gina, I'm so sorry. And Tucker, too." Then he yanked on Annette's hand, to either hurry her along or remind her she wasn't going anywhere if he had anything to do with it.

Sonia had been so overwhelmed by all that was taking place—in particular her husband's much-anticipated apology—she'd initially failed to notice the blood trickling from his left nostril, as well as the purplish-blue swelling under his left eye. Sonia hurried over to him and threw her arms around him after taking Tucker's leash.

Meanwhile, Michael became so lost in the moment as well, he let go of Annette's hand. Naturally she proceeded to make a hasty retreat. No one in the Krumm family appeared to notice what happened, save for Tucker. Nonetheless he didn't attempt to pursue her.

Finally everyone was back together, although the victory was hard-won.

The Ultimate Dog Rescue

Natalie drove her fiancé, Josh, home from the restaurant where they had dinner with his parents. It wasn't the first time Natalie met them nor the first time she had dinner with them. However, this was the first time she'd had to help her fiancé exit the restaurant and get in her vehicle, although he'd arrived separately. His SUV would have to be retrieved in the morning, which wasn't a big deal as far as the distance between the 50-acre ranch where she lived and "The Fireside Log." The problem was Josh would not be pleased to find out his beloved, brand-new black Range Rover was left in the restaurant's parking lot all night. He got so bent out of shape about the most ridiculous things! Between that and his alcoholism, Natalie was seriously reconsidering remaining his fiancée. A huge obstacle was the fact this was a sort of "arranged marriage," and her father would be devastated if she backed out. He was her only parent, as Natalie's mother passed away a couple years ago.

As a commercial real estate agent, Josh worked "unpredictable hours" and liked to combine business meetings with lunch or drinks. Therefore, it shouldn't have been surprising he'd arrived at The Fireside Log almost half an hour late and noticeably intoxicated. Astoundingly, his parents didn't seem to be aware of his condition, even at the end of the evening. Since they had invited Natalie and their son to the restaurant, they paid the bill, but it wasn't like there was any real comfort in as much. There were obviously bigger issues!

Fortunately Natalie wasn't planning on hot, passionate

41

sex tonight. Although Josh was way above average in the looks department, he was a bore in bed. There. The truth. (And another reason not to marry him?)

Even though Josh had stopped by Natalie's on occasion, should he happen to be passing by, he had yet to spend the night. The few times they'd made love, they were at his Phoenix condominium that overlooked "a championship golf course." The living arrangement was far different from what Natalie was accustomed to, and she was in no hurry to change. Her father had made it clear she was welcome to continue her horse training business at the ranch, as long as she wanted. The problem was Josh had no intention of living "far east" of the Phoenix valley. Natalie was willing to compromise and live at his condo and commute back and forth to take care of her horses. However, the biggest problem was the fact her dog Lester hated Josh, and living in a swanky condo with her fiancé was not going to change Lester's mind. At least at the ranch, Lester could avoid Josh, meaning Lester would be spending more time than ever in the barn. That was fine up to a point. Lester liked to sleep next to her bed at night, and he would continue to be allowed to do so, even if Natalie shared her bed with someone else. If the guy had a problem, too bad—even Josh.

Honestly, Natalie was getting way ahead of herself and needed to be concerned with the current dilemma. Having just gotten a good look at Josh "passed out" in the passenger seat of her black Chevy Tahoe, stopped at a light, it was impossible not to wonder how she didn't come unglued, thanks to her pending (and arranged) marriage, alone. It wasn't as if her father said he would disinherit her if she didn't marry this guy. Then again, there was no predicting what her father was really thinking. Unfortunately, the only parent she was close to was her deceased mother. Her passing wasn't entirely unexpected, as she'd been ill, and she'd also been acting strangely—unrelated to her illness. She was the one who "found" Lester for her, as Natalie had suddenly lost her Border Collie, Mandy, who'd run outside the ranch to chase a jackrabbit and in turn was hit by a car. If only there had been a gate at the entrance! As it was, the driver of a sporty black sedan (she couldn't recall the make or model) didn't even stop after the fact.

Sometimes Natalie wished she were a "Daddy's little girl." At least then wouldn't she be more prone to cater to Josh's wishes? One reason she wasn't particularly close to her father was because of him being physically absent, thanks to how much he traveled for his "referral business," whatever that was. All that mattered to Natalie was he made lots of money, enabling her to work at the ranch without having to worry if *she* was making any money!

"Being expected to marry" threw a monkey wrench in Natalie's notion of an ideal life, not just in regard to upsetting her Pembroke Welsh Corgi Lester with the required choice of a husband. She was only twenty-six! Obviously Natalie's father wanted grandkids, which was understandable, but what was the hurry? He never mentioned having any health issues and always said he was fine when she'd ask how he was—which she did every morning. He'd typically call her when she was having breakfast after finishing the barn chores. They never chatted for long, and Natalie accepted the fact her father was simply concerned about her.

Almost back home already, Natalie was anticipating having to pull Josh from the vehicle and drag him in the house. Since her bedroom was closer to the front door and easier to reach than the spare room, he would have to sleep off his hangover in her bed. Natalie (and Lester) would spend the night in the spare bedroom. In the morning she'd drive hungover Josh to "The Fireside Log" to pick up his Range Rover. She was already anticipating having him rag at her about how it was her fault the vehicle was left at the restaurant parking lot all night. He'd recently traded his black BMW sedan for it, and he'd supposedly "loved" that car.

43

The most galling part was Josh's parents had been absolutely no help once they paid the check. Evidently that was the extent of their hospitality for the evening, as their son needed help leaving the restaurant, yet they'd conveniently left beforehand.

At this point, an actual wedding date had not yet been made, so if Josh preferred to just be her boyfriend, she was more than happy to return the beautiful engagement ring. Of course it wasn't as if she wanted to return it, but doing so was only fair. She still craved her personal freedom above all, and there was Lester to keep in mind as well. Arranged marriage or not, the last thing she needed was to be married and miserable. Weren't there already enough people like that?

As it was, Natalie had in fact been engaged once before, to a guy she'd chosen on her own free will, and he turned out to be a liar and a cheater! She actually had her mother to thank for coincidentally having lunch at the same restaurant as Natalie's ex. He was with Tina, his secretary. There was more going on between them than just enjoying a platonic luncheon. Natalie's way of returning the engagement ring Mark gave her (not to be shallow, but it wasn't nearly as impressive as Josh's), was to throw it into busy, six-lane Hayden Road. His architectural firm was at the corner of that road and Via de Ventura. It seemed only appropriate to "catch him at work," in case she could catch him being up to no good with his secretary—who wasn't even very pretty! Wasn't that a prerequisite for being "the other woman"? Admittedly, since Natalie hadn't yet married the guy, maybe she'd overreacted.

Nonetheless, there was no taking back what she did, and Mark almost got hit by a car, attempting to retrieve the ring, swearing at her the entire time. Natalie assumed Tina witnessed her boss/lover, zigzagging across two and a half lanes before abruptly stopping and scooping up the engagement ring. Hopefully he in turn presented Tina with it and proposed as soon as Natalie drove away.

At the ranch, Natalie had to open the metal livestock gate before entering the property. Since she wasn't going back out for the night, the padlock would be locked. The entryway set-up was certainly nothing elaborate, but with the entire ranch fenced, it only made sense to finally have a gate. It was a shame she had to lose her dog Mandy in the meantime. The driver who hit her was a coward for failing to identify himself, which really bothered Natalie. Some sort of punishment was in order if only she knew who it was!

It appeared Josh had passed out beyond waking back up anytime soon, as his head was pushed against the front passenger seat headrest as if he were trying to force it back even further (what a pig!). Given the way he looked at the moment, if he didn't wake up/come to, "taking him in the house" would be more difficult than trying to move a boulder.

Hoping to give herself some advantage, Natalie parked as close to the front stoop as possible. Before even trying to deal with Josh, she would let Lester out. As it was, *he* had no interest in seeing who the overnight lump—or guest—was. Lester was probably right by the door, although he was too polite to scratch on it. Any marks in the wood were courtesy of Mandy.

Sure enough, there Lester was, ecstatic to see Natalie. She petted him, attempting to return some of the affection he gave her. Then she let him out and he headed in the direction of the barn. It wouldn't have been surprising if he "knew" Josh was passed out nearby and wanted to get away.

As soon as Natalie opened the front passenger door, the courtesy light shone right on Josh's face, which looked deathly pale. At first she thought the way his head was tilted made him appear corpse-like. Just as she was about to see if she could wake him with a gentle push, his eyes popped open and he sat up, albeit looking very stiff and uncomfortable. More appropriately he in fact looked dead!

Of course that wasn't possible, and Josh proceeded to exclaim, "Where am I? I need to make a call. Where's my phone?" He appeared to be "thinking aloud," and he wasn't even aware Natalie was standing beside him. As if to confirm as much, he proceeded to suddenly exit the vehicle, forcing her to step back.

Fortunately for Josh, she didn't move far, as he almost fell face-first in the packed sand/gravel driveway, narrowly avoiding the concrete step leading to the front door and stoop. Somehow she managed to grab hold of him in time, the effort requiring more strength than she thought was in her. The extreme anger she secretly felt, must have helped. She even managed to shut the passenger door of the Tahoe.

Hoping to jostle Josh's memory as he continued to attempt standing on his own, Natalie told him, "You're here at my place. We met your parents for dinner earlier this evening, but we'd arrived separately, and you could hardly leave the restaurant, and you'd promised you would forget about your phone for one night!"

Rather than even attempt to reply, Josh simply looked at her, albeit apparently having difficulty focusing. Natalie went on to say, "The plan was for you to spend the night here and not worry about anything else. We'll find your phone and pick up your Range Rover in the morning. Right now you need to get some rest, so help me get you in the house."

Hearing that, Josh looked ready to burst into tears, and it didn't seem like an act. He really was behaving strangely. She told him, "Come on!" in an attempt to get him moving. Otherwise he'd probably end up passing out again, right in the driveway. Another concern was his ghostly pale complexion, which was even more apparent in the dark. The closest light was from a fixture above the front door.

Somehow Natalie was able to guide Josh to her bedroom. Although that sounded romantic, there was nothing sexy about him shuffling along, barely able to keep his balance while maintaining forward motion.

DOGS AND THEIR TWISTED TALES

Natalie's bedroom door was the first one in the hallway, when reached via the front door, after passing through the spacious, Southwestern-themed living room, with oak-paneled walls and wood floor. The spare bedroom was at the end of the hallway, which wasn't long, given the size of the house, but the room could only be reached by a black metal, spiral staircase. Natalie's father had designed this one-and-a-half story, split-log cabin to resemble a ranch hand's rustic abode. Back when there was hired help, the living quarters were in the form of a nondescript-looking, single-wide aluminum trailer that her father had hauled away after Natalie told him it was an eyesore, and she would never need it for any "hired help" because she would do all the work herself.

The loft guest suite was actually Natalie's room when the house was strictly her family's "getaway." Their main house was in the vicinity of Josh's current residence, in the epicenter of the Phoenix valley. As much as she still liked that area, she felt at home in a more rural environment.

Regarding Natalie's father, she only tolerated all the "arranged marriage ridiculousness" because of her respect for him. His dabbling in architecture as a hobby made her all the more impressed with him. Natalie just wished she were referring to her fiancé. At the moment she essentially had no respect for him.

The second Josh was by the bed, he started to pass out, so Natalie conveniently positioned him to fall onto it. All she had to do was move his lower legs so they weren't hanging over the side.

It was a huge relief having Josh situated for the time being. Since Natalie figured he wasn't going anywhere for awhile, she removed his brown leather dress loafers and loosened his tie. Granted, he probably didn't care, he was so out of it. Not to be selfish, but as far as his shoes, she very simply didn't want them on her zebra-striped comforter.

Taking one last look at Josh before turning off the light and shutting the bedroom door—but careful not to lock it—

Natalie couldn't help shaking her head. Enough of him! It was time to get Lester in, the real love of her life. That was a terrible thing to say when her fiancé was passed out in her bedroom. On second thought, it made perfect sense.

Lester was waiting right outside the front door, eager to come inside. As Natalie was double locking the door, he went ahead and tried to go straight to bed, to no avail. Then she realized his bed was in there. Retrieving it most likely wouldn't awaken Josh, so she'd go ahead and sneak back inside. Given his condition she probably didn't even need to be furtive.

Expectantly, Lester looked up as Natalie started to turn the doorknob, which was locked! That was practically impossible. After all, what were the chances Josh "came to" long enough to lock her out? Rather than obsess over the possibility, she'd worry about it in the morning.

Before falling asleep in the royal blue silk pants and shirt she wore to dinner, Natalie realized she didn't have her alarm clock! She'd have to count on Lester to wake her up. As it was, she was so exhausted it was possible she'd oversleep, which happened occasionally, even with the alarm clock.

Natalie awoke to the sound of Lester shaking his head and body, making his rabies and identification tags loudly jingle. She told him, "All right, I hear you! We'll go out in a minute." She felt rested in a way but at the same time was more exhausted than ever. Then last night's debacle came back to her.

The first order of business involved letting Lester out, and afterward Natalie would check on Josh. Hopefully the bedroom door was no longer locked—if it really ever was.

After some hesitation regarding descending the spiral metal staircase, Lester was finally persuaded to do so and looked proud of himself afterward.

Once Lester was outside, via the back (kitchen) door, Natalie went to see Josh. Even though she was "worried" the door might still be locked, she wasn't particularly worried about Josh. That sounded terrible, but it was true.

This time the door not only wasn't locked, it turned too easily, as if Josh was turning the knob, too. Natalie asked, "Josh, are you awake?" and looked in the direction of the bed. It faced directly away from the doorway, so she couldn't see him. His shoes were by the bed, exactly where she'd placed them last night, but it didn't appear he was still in bed. The only other place he could be was the bathroom, but the door was open and it was dark in there.

Jonathan Pershing, Natalie's father, was frankly worried as hell about his daughter. It was unheard of for her to fail to answer the phone in the morning. He'd call her around 7:30 or a quarter to eight and chat with her for a couple minutes. She was alone at what was technically "his" ranch, and she did all the work herself. At least she had her dog, Lester, to keep her company. He was a sort of gift from her mother, Madeleine, Jonathan's beloved wife, who'd passed away. She'd gotten the Corgi through a private rescue for which she volunteered. At times Madeleine annoyed Jonathan with her dedication, as he wanted her home to make dinner, yet she was busy delivering a Pembroke or Cardigan Corgi to a new home, sometimes a state or two away. The thing was, Madeleine was always a homebody and didn't even like to drive! He happened to travel quite a bit himself, so when he was home, he wanted his wife at home too. Jonathan was all for Madeleine's charity efforts, but since he provided very well for her, he wanted his stipulation obeyed and as much should have been understood.

Natalie had unexpectedly lost her Border Collie, a shelter dog, so acquiring another rescue was inevitable, but she was in no hurry. Unfortunately it appeared Natalie was almost resentful about having another dog so soon, which really hurt her mother's feelings.

Doreen Shale was "an eccentric friend from high school"

who'd established a private dog rescue, coincidentally primarily for Corgis. If Madeleine wasn't best friends with Doreen in their teen years, she appeared to be so in adulthood. Madeleine in fact acted like there was nothing she wouldn't do for Doreen, as if she were under a spell.

O.K., the truth: It seemed like Madeleine became possessed, the longer she volunteered at her friend Doreen's dog rescue. As it was, Madeleine hadn't even owned a dog since she was young. Natalie had gotten her Border Collie because she was living alone at the ranch and was lonely (although she'd never admit it). When the three of them had used the ranch as a getaway, it would have been logical to have a dog, but Natalie was so caught up in her horses, she didn't care. Madeleine didn't want to bother with a dog no one cared about—which included Jonathan, not that he had anything whatsoever against dogs or their owners.

Natalie was in fact so obsessed with horses, it didn't seem like she'd ever care about anything else (like marriage and kids). It frankly worried Jonathan, just how single-minded his only child was, which was the number one reason he'd agreed to having Natalie be a part of an "arranged marriage." It wasn't a written-in-stone kind of situation, but it was close, if only to maintain Jonathan's integrity. Not to be selfish, but he'd worked hard to attain his level of prosperity, and the rest of his family had prospered as well.

Josh Melbourne was "the chosen mate," a commercial real estate agent, and his parents, Martin and Ann, acted like he was the s**t, which was aided by the fact he was an only child, just like Natalie. One issue Jonathan and Madeleine had agreed on, was to be very conservative raising their only child, and that included not spoiling her. Jonathan liked to think Madeleine and he did pretty well. Or maybe they stayed far enough out of the way, was all. Overall Natalie was so unassuming.

Although Jonathan had met Josh, they had yet to spend even a few minutes together. Something always came up for one or the other, so there was never an opportunity for them to go out (with Natalie). However, the Melbournes had taken Josh and their future daughter-in-law out on a few occasions. The first time they did so, Jonathan felt like they'd done him a favor, as in at least *they* were showing their support. Then, as time passed, he came to realize he was not only leaving himself out of the equation, he was ambivalent about the "arranged marriage." There was no telling what Natalie really thought.

Jonathan admired both Madeleine and Doreen's dedication to a worthy cause, but in regard to the former, her attitude made no sense. Since Doreen never married nor had kids, saving dogs had obviously become her life, hence her obsession.

One evening shortly after Madeleine had "presented" Natalie with Lester (and she was none too happy about her daughter's reaction to "the gift"), she'd mentioned to Jonathan, "You know, sometimes I wonder. I mean, I think maybe Doreen has a sixth sense or something. I'm actually kind of afraid of her." Then she emitted a strange-sounding laugh, which he'd never before heard in the close to thirty years they'd been married.

Jonathan was creeped-out for a few seconds. At the same time, he could tell Madeleine was very upset about Natalie's indifference to her new dog, so he did his best to console his wife. Despite his best intentions, she remained preoccupied.

The logical thing for Jonathan to do was go to the ranch and check on Natalie, so that was where he was headed. He was also "dressed for work," in one of his expensive tailored suits, as he was going to the office afterward, even though it was in the opposite direction.

Stopped at a light about halfway to the ranch, Jonathan tried calling Natalie, but there was no answer. Naturally he became more agitated than ever, and once the light changed, he took off like he was in a race. Fortunately he was aware he was speeding before a cop had to point out as much.

Arriving at the ranch, Jonathan was stopped short at the entrance because there was a padlocked, metal livestock gate! This was what he got for not visiting Natalie more and keeping up on matters. He sure as hell didn't have a key to unlock the padlock. It was worth a try to call her cell phone again, maybe she'd finally answer.

Nothing. Natalie's Tahoe was parked perpendicular to the front stoop of the house, that much Jonathan could see, peering between the gate's steel tubing. She had to be home, although she did meet Josh and his parents for dinner at "The Fireside Log." Possibly Josh took Natalie back to his place for the night, but it wasn't like her to fail to return in time for her early-morning chores. It was nine o'clock, so she should have been back. If necessary she'd walk the twenty miles, should he refuse to give her a ride home, as she'd be too stubborn to call a cab.

With that possibility in mind, Jonathan got back in his Mercedes SUV and started it, only to realize how ridiculous it would be to go looking for his daughter. He forgave himself for as much, only because the idea had been entirely stress-induced.

What Jonathan first needed to do was confirm Natalie wasn't anywhere on the property before taking off to look for her. This meant he'd have to access the place by climbing the steel gate. It was impossible to climb the tall, wire-mesh fencing that surrounded the entire ranch, not that the gate appeared exactly inviting, especially given how he was dressed.

His keys secured in a buttoned suit coat pocket, Jonathan began climbing the gate. As soon as he was at the top, precariously straddling it, his phone rang! He'd never thought to secure it and wasn't sure where it was, despite its ringing. Carefully he checked his left front pants pocket and located it, all the while precariously balancing on the top of the gate. Assuming the caller was Natalie, Jonathan would risk losing his balance to answer the phone, so he shifted it to his right hand, simultaneously attempting to confirm the number. Barely two seconds later he lost his balance and the phone went flying. It landed right behind the right front tire of his Mercedes, while he ended up inside the property, although his left leg was caught between two of the gate rungs, causing him to scream in pain.

While quickly working to free his wrenched leg and foot, Jonathan couldn't help wondering if Natalie had heard him but assumed she was imagining things. He could only wish *he* was.

Also, where was Lester? Natalie claimed the dog was very protective of her and the ranch. Fortunately the animal liked Jonathan, so there wouldn't be a stand-off between them. At least, he didn't think.

Jonathan's foot finally free, it hurt like hell, along with his leg and hip. Also, he was acquiring a terrific headache. His prescription migraine pills were in his vehicle, so that naturally meant they might as well have been miles away. Maybe it was just as well, as they made him drowsy. He'd imagine having taken one, and hopefully the headache would go away. Admittedly, once a headache set in, its pain cancelled out any other pain sources.

Letting Natalie "just keep living at the ranch" after her mother died was a lousy idea. Madeleine often cooked for her and would take the meals to the ranch while paying a visit – all of which happened several times a week, even after Madeleine became Doreen Shale's guinea pig, gofer, slave ... dog? Which noun was the most appropriate?

Madeleine never did answer Jonathan's question: "Does Doreen's 'private rescue' even have an actual name or is it 'private-private' and isn't even technically a charity, just her way of doing something financially self-serving, on someone else's dime?"

It was obviously too late to feel regrets; Jonathan felt he was successful because of vowing to emotionally move forward NO MATTER WHAT. Nor would he ever waver on that credo. Even though he couldn't cook, he would visit Natalie more and could take her out to lunch or dinner – if she could tear herself away from the ranch long enough to do so. At this point she didn't have to marry that Josh-fellow if she wasn't comfortable with the situation.

Meanwhile, Jonathan would prepare to cut back on his workload and the amount of traveling he did. As much as he hated to delegate responsibilities, it wasn't as if there weren't any capable employees to help shoulder his workload. By this time in his life he could literally afford to slow down, but he'd never stopped long enough to contemplate doing so!

Therefore, Jonathan had managed to put "a positive spin" on an unfortunate predicament! As an already successful businessman, it proved he still had what it took and was at the top of his game. It was hard not to gloat sometimes.

Jonathan must have in fact dozed off because he suddenly awoke to a dog, licking his face! "Ugh! Get away!" he screamed, waving his arms, which resulted in him unintentionally hitting both his hands against the steel gate. It was completely inexcusable he fell asleep, no matter the circumstances.

Anyway, there was a dog staring at him while keeping its distance, and it wasn't Lester. Natalie must have adopted another Corgi. Jonathan wasn't up on his daughter's personal life, despite briefly chatting with her every morning, so this was a surprise.

Feeling guilty for having scared the dog away, Jonathan said, "I'm sorry for having overreacted, doggie. I'm not a 'dog-person,' so you'll have to forgive me."

In turn, the dog appeared less anxious and proceeded to sit on its haunches, a couple feet away, still closely watching him. Or was he imagining as much? Then again, it was more like there was something familiar in its quizzical expression. All in all, the whole situation was becoming more and more bizarre.

Even more strange, Jonathan found himself asking the dog, "Where's my daughter, Natalie? And her dog, Lester? Surely you know *him*!" Then he had to laugh because he was talking to a dog – and asking it questions! Did that automatically make him a dog-person?

"The dog" proceeded to leap up and start trotting in the direction of the house, continuously looking back at Jonathan, as if he were expected to follow. Hopefully a door was unlocked, since he didn't have a key, although there was one back at his house. At this point he was only concerned with Natalie's well-being, and he assumed this unfamiliar dog was trying to lead him to her. Not to feel sorry for himself, but he lost his wife to a rather sudden illness, and she'd been the love of his life. Already it'd been two years, and he couldn't imagine meeting a woman for a simple "coffee date." The bottom line was he wondered why anything ever went right. That kind of thinking compelled him to seek professional help, but he was certain his problems would be solved if he spent more time with Natalie, despite her determination she craved solitude.

The front door was unlocked, so Jonathan went ahead and pushed it open, only to have "the dog" sneak in and disappear.

"Hey!" Jonathan exclaimed, unable to help himself. What was it about that dog? Obviously it did something to him.

Peering around the living room, he called, "Natalie? Natalie!" There was a rush of cold air, and Jonathan felt as if it literally pushed him toward the hallway leading to the bedrooms. There was also a second-story guest suite, which was his daughter's, growing up. Having designed the house himself, he couldn't help but be proud of his accomplishment, if only because it proved he had a creative side. Despite his business acumen, Jonathan felt insecure regarding whether he was sufficiently "well-rounded" as a person. He hated the thought of being considered one-dimensional.

That was Jonathan Pershing's last thought in the dimension known as being a human.

It was Doreen Shale's lucky day when a former classmate from high school, approached her to volunteer at Doreen's dog rescue (which openly favored Corgis). Madeleine Fritz (her maiden name) always was easy to tell what to do, and she hadn't changed. Whatever a man saw in a groveling sap like her was anyone's guess. Then again, Doreen never married because she gave up finding a man who could put up with her "my way or the highway" mentality, just like they had.

Enough about herself. The important point was Doreen had inherited not only a sizable estate from her parents, she inherited some "unique talents" she had only lately discovered, coincidentally not until after she'd started her Corgi rescue. Initially she'd welcomed any dog, any age, although she'd been limited by the size of her shelter accommodation. Then she realized it was in her power to eliminate annoying, cloying, complaining people who had it made and turn them into none other than Pembroke and Cardigan Welsh Corgis!

So far there appeared to be just one problem: once Doreen "cast her spell," it spread like a contagion. Doreen hadn't meant to subject Madeleine's family to this "experiment," but they had it coming to them. Sadly, Madeleine had become very ill with a rare form of cancer in the meantime, and it was undoubtedly due to how her husband and daughter took her for granted. Madeleine even adopted a Corgi named Lester, to give to her daughter, who'd let her other dog run in the street, who was fatally hit by a car. Whoever was driving the vehicle deserved to get his, one way or another.

Anyway, the longer Madeleine had volunteered at Doreen's Corgi rescue, the more compelled she was to talk about her family. It was evident she loved her husband,

Jonathan, and their only child, Natalie. At the same time, Jonathan appeared to travel practically nonstop for his business, even though he had the means to delegate far more responsibilities than he did. As for twenty-something Natalie, she sounded like a reclusive, horse-obsessed loner who was living at the family ranch, essentially mooching off her parents. Why not? Evidently neither parent cared to deliver any sort of ultimatum, although supposedly she worked hard and didn't have any hired help.

At this point, Doreen had a responsibility: to do a well-being check on Madeleine's daughter and take things from there. The packed sand and stone driveway was within view, as she'd just turned right off Shea Boulevard, onto Painted Desert Drive. "Painted Desert Ranch" was the name of the Pershings' place, and Madeleine was proud of the fact the street was named after their property, not the other way around. From what little Doreen was able to discern thus far, it was a rustic but classy place. Madeleine had made no secret about her love for it and had described it in such detail (including the address), there was no difficulty finding it.

Noticing there was a silver Mercedes SUV parked in front of the livestock gate, barring the entrance, Doreen felt queasy. When she saw the license plate read "JBP," her heart sank. That had to be Jonathan Pershing's vehicle. His wife died of cancer and their daughter, their only child, along with him, were turned into . . .

As quickly as she could, Doreen ran to the right side of the driveway and threw up. Afterward she dry-heaved several times. She felt terrible—mentally more than anything. However, there was no undoing what had already been done. The spell had been cast, which was literally true in this instance.

Doreen's plan of action still hadn't changed; she needed to check on Natalie. Whatever happened to Natalie's father, Doreen would have to take things as they came. That included entering the property. Since the gate was locked, it would have to be scaled.

Just as Doreen was about to put her right foot on the bottom rung of the gate, a black Audi SUV pulled up right behind her van. All she could think was how inconsiderate the driver was. However, it was imperative she keep her cool. Otherwise she ran the risk of giving herself away . . . Then again, whatever was happening was so unbelievable, it created the perfect cover.

Taking charge of the situation, Doreen asked the obviously-moneyed couple as they simultaneously exited their vehicle, "Can I help you folks?"

The wife looked at the husband, who answered, "To be honest, I'm not sure. We're Josh Melbourne's parents, who's Natalie Pershing's fiancé. We're nearly certain he spent the night here because he left 'The Fireside Log' with her. At least, we *think* so. We left before them but we paid the bill! Anyway, Josh's new Range Rover is still in the restaurant parking lot, and leaving it there isn't something he would willingly allow, not by this time of the morning. He's crazy about that thing, just like he was about his BMW, until he accidentally hit a stray dog with it."

Doreen almost felt sorry for this family until hearing about their son "accidentally" hitting a dog. It was anyone's guess if the animal was actually a stray or not. Why assume you knew?

Bolstered by all this, Doreen told the elder Melbournes (who were so rude they couldn't be bothered to give their first names), "*I'm* actually here to check on Natalie, as well as her father. I'm a family friend. I was very close to Madeleine. I don't have a key to the gate because I left it at home, so we'll have to climb it and check things out. Hopefully nothing's amiss." She only lied about having a key to the gate, so there.

Watching Mr. and Mrs. Melbourne awkwardly climb the gate, their clumsiness partially hindered by their inappropriate dress (both looked beach-ready in their shorts, tank-tops and flip-flops), Doreen couldn't help but smile. It made no difference she didn't know their first names; once they were adopted, they'd have new ones. And there was a "Corgi waiting list," including for an older, widowed resident in Tucson who wanted one last Pembroke before she passed away. Her wish would be fulfilled by tomorrow afternoon. Doreen would personally make the delivery.

Amy Kristoff

Petie's O.K. After All

Andie knew exactly what *really* happened to her dog, Petie, but her parents had no idea she knew. If she weren't so upset, the whole situation would have been an opportunity for some fun. There never seemed to be much opportunity for that because her parents were always arguing, especially lately. The night before they'd done some preparing for "a long trip," and Andie was instructed to pack "her favorite clothes and toys" in a single large suitcase. Andie suspected they were never coming back, especially since their biggest argument involved not keeping up with THE MORTGAGE. Meanwhile she stupidly thought Petie would be coming with them.

About three-thirty this morning, Andie was awakened by her mother and was told they were leaving on this "trip" in thirty minutes. Just like that! Looking back (by a couple hours), she should have made a run for it, right then and there. She could have rescued Petie on her way out, as one parent or the other had left him tied to the enormous maple tree by the road, about the only tree on the flat, ten-acre property. Andie would really miss the place. Both her parents always talked like they were afraid of THE MORTGAGE, and it turned out they had reason to be. Her mom never had a job, as far as Andie knew, and her father always called his boss an "S-O-B." Andie's best friend, Wendy Dell, didn't even have a dad—or he didn't live with Wendy and her mom. And her mother only had to "pay rent," which her boss paid most of the time! That whole situation seemed to make more sense than Andie's. The only problem was, the apartment complex where Wendy and her mom lived, didn't allow any pets. Wendy didn't care because she was obsessed with horses. Meanwhile, Andie was obsessed with Petie. She was certain he loved her, unlike her selfish parents. She owed it to Petie to return home and untie him. It would be the second time he was rescued, as her family had adopted him from the Cook County Animal Shelter in Greenwood, Illinois. It was the same town her family had lived in. It was less than an hour from downtown Chicago, where her father used to work, in one of those tall buildings. Or so he said. Anymore, Andie didn't trust her parents, and she hated them from this point on.

When George Sterley left for work this morning, his wife, Vicki, was in bed, fast asleep. That wasn't unusual, as he had to leave the house about 4:45, to pick up his truck at South Suburban Waste Company's main garage. However, she'd had a problem when she was going through her divorce (from her ex-husband): sleepwalking! She never went much farther than wherever she was sleeping, but it nonetheless freaked her out after the fact.

Even though George drove the same waste pick-up routes every week, he never failed to see something different. In other words he never got bored. He'd driven one kind of truck or another for a living since he was nineteen, and this job was by far the best one overall. The ultimate job security was knowing there would always be garbage.

And at the end of the Mellados' long, narrow, paved driveway, there sat the plastic waste container, overflowing with bags of garbage. That was definitely unusual for this family. They only had one kid, he was pretty sure. Maybe they finally cleaned out their garage or a spare room. Then he noticed the plywood sign, nailed to the enormous maple tree. In black block letters it read: PLEASE TAKE OUR PETIE. WE HAD TO LEAVE. HE IS THREE YEARS OLD, NEUTERED

Amy Kristoff

AND A MIX OF DACHSHUND AND A TERRIER OF SOME KIND. THANK YOU FOR CARING.

After reading the sign several times, still in his truck, George finally looked down and saw "Petie," who was tied to the tree trunk by a very long, thick, white cotton rope. George knew next to nothing about dogs, but one that didn't chew through a leash that was keeping him in place, was a damned good dog because of that alone.

Well-aware it was completely against company policy to pick up a dog, any dog, George was actually considering doing so. Ever since his wife lost her dearly beloved "Buddy," she was adamant she didn't want another dog, ever. In the meantime, she was absolutely miserable. She had even started working again, at a veterinary clinic, to help her stay busy and allow her to be around animals. His only reservation was giving her an unwanted surprise. Maybe she was still too heartbroken, although it had been at least six months since Buddy died. George hated to admit it, but he never knew what love was until meeting Vicki. He was her second husband and she was his second wife. His ex, Tammy, was pure hell, but he tried to love her anyway. Fortunately they never had kids, sad though that was to declare.

Lost in thought and not doing his job, George would be running late, which would cut into his lunch break. He liked to stop at "Deb's Diner" in tiny Granite, Illinois. The restaurant was close to the railroad tracks, and he liked how it seemed the whole building shook whenever a train passed. In the meantime "Petie" was staring right at him, and having finally noticed as much, George about cried! And he could have counted on one hand, how many times he'd cried in his entire life. In other words he wasn't the most sentimental guy, but this dog was stirring his soul.

Dry water bowl and long cotton rope in tow, Petie was carefully placed on the passenger seat of the garbage truck. The hell with South Suburban's policy. Although George had to keep his route, after lunch he happened to pass within a few miles of Vicki's and his place, so he could make a quick detour and drop Petie off. Vicki was at work until 5:30 or even 6:00 on Tuesdays, so George would be home for the day first and could explain Petie's presence.

Already a couple miles from the Mellados', George had stopped a few times for garbage pick-ups before it occurred to him he should have removed the sign for Petie. After exchanging a look with the dog, he decided that wasn't important. Petie had his new home, and the former owners obviously expected a good Samaritan to come along. There was no one else who was relevant to the situation at this point. Right?

Anymore, everything seemed out of sync. Vicki never would have burdened her husband, George, by voicing her anxiety, but she felt like being fifty-two was really dragging her down. Aging (and menopause) had turned out to be even worse than she'd anticipated. Everything had to be just so or she was ruined for the day, like she had a major case of O.C.D.

One thing Vicki couldn't leave the house without doing in the morning was having breakfast. Meanwhile, George preferred to skip it and have lunch most weekdays at a favorite dining spot. It wasn't as if she wouldn't have gladly gotten up and made him breakfast (and then gone back to sleep until it was time for work, shortly afterward). In other words, she loved him, which was a comfort. When going through her divorce, Vicki had started sleepwalking (again) because she was so anxious. It was embarrassing to tell George she had this problem, although she appeared to have overcome it by the time they'd married. Ever since losing her beloved dog, "Buddy," six months ago, however, she'd feared having a sleepwalking episode or two. As it was, she'd vowed not to get another dog because losing him to cancer had been so heartbreaking. If it hadn't been for Buddy, she not only wouldn't have made it through her divorce, she wouldn't have been able to cope with living alone, as both her kids were already out of the house by that time. Vicki was presented with Buddy after revealing to her friend Denise, a devoted dog-person, she was stressed-out; she had a spacious, fenced yard; and she had many positive memories of dog ownership in her youth. It was amazing her kids never clamored for a dog. Maybe it had to do with the fact they always managed to occupy themselves with various activities.

Fortunately, Vicki "won" her house in the divorce settlement. Even better, the mortgage was paid. That had allowed her to work or take time off, and she could "afford" to be choosy about what she did. At times, a job was just a job, but the one she currently had, working at "Andover Animal Hospital," was definitely more than a job because it was also a form of therapy. Her only complaint was it didn't appear she'd be cured of her "ailment" (heartbreak from losing Buddy) anytime soon. She didn't want another dog, but her life felt so empty without one. It was just as well her kids were clueless about dog ownership; nowadays they had their careers to nurture, instead.

When Vicki said she would have gotten up extra-early to make her husband breakfast and then gone back to sleep, only to have to get back up shortly afterward, it only seemed like barely any time passed. As it was, Tuesday was the only morning she had to show up at the clinic at 7:00 A.M., to help with the first responsibilities of the day.

On this particular Tuesday, Vicki turned off the alarm, went back to sleep and almost overslept. If she wanted breakfast before leaving for work, there wasn't much time. And she didn't get off until 5:30 at the earliest on Tuesdays, her longest working day of the week. She worked just as late Wednesdays and Thursdays, but she didn't start until noon. Working late was the perfect excuse not to have to cook, so she'd pick up dinner three nights a week, usually at "Ted's

Carry-Out," which was near the animal hospital.

Vicki ended up leaving the house without breakfast and planned on picking up fast food. Never before had she been late to any job for any reason, and she wasn't going to do so today, if only as a matter of principle. At the same time, it wasn't like she had a problem with fast food; she simply preferred to enjoy breakfast at home.

Andie could not believe her good fortune. Her father finally stopped at a rest stop and it was one of those two-way ones. Even better, both her parents had fallen asleep, sitting in the car! "All" she had to do was walk over to the other side of the tan brick building where the restrooms were and find someone to take her home. She was in the restroom once already with her mother. On their way out, Andie asked if she could have a package of peanut butter crackers from one of the vending machines, only to be tersely told, "We'll sit down together tonight and eat in a restaurant." They'd already missed breakfast because Andie's father drove until he couldn't stay awake. The car had to be about out of gas, so they'd have to stop again. Why couldn't they eat then? Was THE MORTGAGE chasing them? It sure seemed like it. Andie was hungry and ready for lunch by this time. If her mother had driven her car as well, maybe *they* could have stopped to eat—and just maybe Petie could have joined them on this "trip" after all.

On her way to the parking area on the opposite side of the brick building, Andie looked back at her parents' station wagon several times, making sure they had no idea she was leaving. If either one did suddenly wake up and come after her, she'd simply say she had to use the restroom again. The problem was her parents were so unpredictable anymore, along with being paranoid.

Despite her parents' "order" not to ever talk to strangers, Andie intended to do just that, all so she could return home and (hopefully) rescue Petie from being tied to the tree in front of her house. He was probably hungry too by this time, even if her parents were considerate enough to feed him breakfast before deserting him.

Tapped on her left shoulder, Andie was awakened from daydreaming and turned around, expecting to see her mother intently staring at her. The stare had been perfected thanks to Andie's father, who'd come home from work later and later and often blamed as much on his boss, whom he couldn't stand. Meanwhile, Andie's mother didn't buy any of his excuses for always being late.

Andie found herself looking at the brass belt buckle of an older man with a salt-and-pepper beard and mustache. She hesitated to make eye contact but when she did, it was like his eyes were super-big and unbelievably round. She didn't notice what color they were because she was suddenly very afraid. Then he smiled, revealing several bottom teeth that were crooked and rotten-looking. While Andie fixated on his mouth, the man asked her, "You lookin' for somebody, pretty little girl?"

Emboldened by her desire to be reunited with Petie, Andie told the stranger, "I need to find someone who's on their way to Greenwood, Illinois. My parents made me leave the house we had there, but they left our dog Petie. I have to get home to him right away."

The man agreed, no questions asked! Instead of feeling somewhat relieved, Andie felt worse, especially when he grabbed her wrist and warned her not to scream "or else." Then he led her toward a large moving van. The only words she noticed were: "Worldwide Elite Moving Services." All she could think was how badly she only wanted to go home to her dog, not take a trip around the world. With that she started to cry.

Glancing at Petie while driving to his lunch stop, George was impressed with how comfortable the dog was, given what the little guy had already been through. George felt such a kinship with Petie, he asked him, "You need a bathroom break and drink of water?" Even though it was unbelievable he, George, was talking to a dog, he went on to say, "I'm gonna have a quick lunch and read the paper. I'll get some water for you and then we'll go to a park for a few minutes."

George was so moved by his feelings for Petie, he had goose bumps. This was ridiculous, yet he didn't care. In fact, he felt stupid for having failed to appreciate his wife's dog, Buddy, when the dog was part of the household.

Parking his garbage truck in the back of Deb's Diner's gravel parking lot, George remembered to leave both the driver's side and passenger windows opened slightly. It was the middle of June, but it wasn't hot, and the sky was mostly cloudy.

"I'll be right back, furry friend," George told Petie and headed for the restaurant. He even looked back once, to see if the dog was watching him. Meanwhile, George would sit at a table by one of the windows that overlooked the parking lot. Sometimes he sat at the counter, mostly because that was where an already-read newspaper could be found. Since he had lunch around eleven, the restaurant was usually empty. Anyone present was a holdover from breakfast.

Helping expedite matters, the service in the diner was extremely efficient. His favorite waitress was Tracy, a petite thirty-something with light brown hair. She was always nearby to refill his coffee cup. Even though he didn't have a long break, he usually managed to drink three cups. On this particular day, he'd have to limit himself to one or two cups – and he'd need a cup of water "to go."

Barely had George sat down in a booth by the far east window of the restaurant, and someone backed his office furniture delivery truck right up next to George's truck, blocking George's view of it. He would have to make his lunch break even more brief. The amazing part was his concern for Petie.

The plastic-coated menus were wedged between the napkin holder and the salt and pepper shakers. George had a look at the menu, even though he had the thing memorized. With breakfast served all day, he opted for the relatively simple order of fried eggs over easy with toast.

Around eleven, Vicki became nauseous. Even if she couldn't blame her sudden illness on her fast food breakfast, she would do so anyway. It was her fault she'd overslept, uprooting her schedule. She had just helped Doctor Helena Meeker with an emergency surgery for a big, rangy, tan-haired mutt named Ramsey, who was kicked in the front left leg by a horse.

Once Ramsey had sufficiently awakened from his surgery and was resting, Vicki would be able to take her lunch break. Since she only had a half-hour, it wasn't worth it to go home, although there were a few shortcuts to take. Given how Vicki felt, however, she not only needed to go home, she probably wasn't going to be back for the rest of the day. She must have looked convincing because barely did she explain herself, and Doctor Meeker sent her on her way.

Abigail awoke with a start, initially wondering where she was, until the crick in her neck jostled her memory. To her left was her pathetic husband, Paul, fast asleep. They were parked at a rest stop, a few hours from home. At a time like this, he should have been driving like hell, to get them to their destination, some remote town in Texas or New Mexico, she wasn't sure which, where his parents owned a rental that needed fixing up before the new tenants moved in. Obviously "the new tenants" would be the three of them, and they were expected to clean the place up, in exchange for staying there for nothing. What a change for a man who had been "a higher-up" at the financial institution that had employed him. On this "trip," Abigail had plenty of time to think about her family's circumstances, and she found it entirely unacceptable, Paul not only "lost his job," there wasn't enough money in their bank account to pay the mortgage while he looked for new employment. Meanwhile, she'd stayed home all day and only left to run errands or go to the supermarket. In other words, if there wasn't enough money, he was the one spending it as fast as he made it. Both of them had been driving cars that were over a decade old. (But at least they were paid for.) Formerly Paul made very good money. Otherwise Abigail would have gotten a job. At the same time, it wasn't like she minded being a stay-at-home mom. There was always something to do, and she had their dog, Petie, to keep her company. What a trouper! Her heart broke, thinking about what Paul made her do to Petie before they left home for good. As shitty as his parents' rental probably was, they were adamant a dog was not allowed, not even for their son and his family! As much as Abigail believed in respecting her marriage vows, being forced to leave Petie behind was about the last straw. The most ridiculous part was Paul had refused to let her take Petie back to the animal shelter where they'd adopted him. Instead she had to tie him to the only tree on the property, coincidentally by the road. Also, she posted a sign, briefly describing Petie and essentially soliciting someone to take him home. If nothing else, maybe the garbage man would take pity on the poor dog.

Finally, Abigail looked in the back seat of the Volvo station wagon, expecting to see her daughter, Andie, napping. Instead she wasn't even there! She looked at Paul again and noticed he was drooling. That really said it all.

Abigail exited the passenger side of the car and headed for the restrooms. She expected to find Andie there, even though they both used the facilities right after Paul parked at the two-way rest stop, complaining he couldn't stay awake (but he wouldn't let Abigail drive, knowing she'd turn around and go back home). She didn't even know where they were. Hopefully they'd at least made it out of Illinois.

On her way up the concrete walkway to the restroom building, Abigail recalled her daughter wanting a package of peanut butter and crackers from one of the vending machines but had been told "no," in so many words. Andie had probably scraped together some loose change she found in the back seat and finally got her crackers. Abigail teared up at the notion; with all that was going on, this was no time to be absurdly strict with Andie. As it was, she too had to be devastated Petie was left behind. (Paul assumed their daughter wouldn't care about the family dog.)

This was amazing. George was referring to how enamored he was, just observing Petie, strolling slightly ahead of him on the sidewalk that encircled Shaeffer Park. The park encompassed about an acre, and most of it was shaded by huge oak trees. The small back yards of houses surrounded the park, with a four-foot-high cyclone fence dividing the public and private property. Since George and Petie had the place to themselves, it was especially peaceful. The long cotton rope was serving its purpose as a leash, but as soon as George got him home, it would no longer be used. Even though Vicki declared she never wanted another dog after Buddy, she still had all the supplies. (She had his collar wrapped around a brass container with a paw print on the lid, containing his ashes, as he was cremated.) To top it off she appeared to be miserable despite attempting to "move on," acting as if she didn't have time for a dog. Working at a vet clinic was only making matters worse, which was understandable for any number of reasons. Also, she had empty nest syndrome, something she would never admit, only because she simultaneously knew it was selfish not to be happy for her kids, having left home to attend college and have careers in the film industry on the West Coast.

"Come on, let's go back to the truck," George told Petie. "I'm taking you home. I just have to make a couple more stops. But don't tell my boss I'm doing this."

Talking to Petie was already turning into a habit, and George was finding he liked it. What was there not to like?

DOGS AND THEIR TWISTED TALES

***

While Abigail and her husband looked around the rest stop for their daughter, she was repeatedly warned by him not to appear desperate. Initially it was difficult for her to follow such a ridiculous "order," but before too long she sunk into such despair it was actually easy not to look desperate. Simply put: she was in shock. Meanwhile, Paul had to be going through the same thing, as he kept walking back and forth between the two rest stop parking lots – one for the northbound and southbound traffic. Or was it eastbound and westbound? Abigail honestly did not know! Admittedly she fell asleep at least once or twice while Paul was driving. She'd vowed to stay awake and help him stay awake, but part of the problem was the fact she was disgusted with him for basically running away from their life yet refused to offer any explanation. She happened to think that "being married" meant "being able to communicate with your spouse." Paul used to be at least willing to listen to her, even if he never did open up much. Abigail had learned to accept the situation, but in the past six months, Paul had really closed himself off. Looking back, she wished she would have delivered him an ultimatum: we go to counseling or we split up. Forcing Paul to talk to a stranger would have scared him into finally talking to his wife. At least it would have been worth a try.

Abigail went back to the women's restroom, this time because she had to use the facilities. She'd already looked for Andie in here so many times it was ridiculous. Initially Paul kept telling Abigail to come in here; after awhile she came in here to get away from him. At this point, Andie probably wasn't at the rest stop at all!

With that Abigail burst into tears.

There was more than one shortcut home, so Vicki randomly picked one. Her goal was to make it home before she

71

became so ill it was necessary to stop. Fortunately the cho-
sen shortcut involved rural roads, as she would be cutting
through the environs of Greenwood, which was very small.
The town limits were wedged between the town limits of
Andover, which comprised an inverse U-shape. Andover
Animal Hospital, where Vicki worked, was on one side, while
George and she lived on the other, in a rural area.

Vicki made it about halfway home and happened to be on
150th Street in Greenwood when she became so nauseous
it was imperative to pull over and turn off the ignition. To
the right of her Subaru, there was a five-acre parcel offered
for sale by a local real estate company. Her car happened to
be parked even with the sign, so she could pretend to be
looking at the property, not that there would be a vehicle
passing by in either direction for a few minutes. That was
how quiet the road appeared to be.

Just as Vicki was about to get back in her car, she
noticed a plywood sign across the road, posted on a huge
tree. (The tree looked especially large because it was the only
one around, as all the five and ten-acre properties around
here were developed on former cropland.) On the sign Vicki
read "a mix of dachshund and a terrier" in black block letters, and she completely forgot about feeling ill and hurried
across the street. Then she noticed the dark green plastic
waste container for South Suburban Waste Company, the
name of George's employer.

Since the container was empty, George had to have been
here. However, it was impossible he took Petie, who must
have been tied to the tree. First of all, George was at best
indifferent about dogs. He sure was toward Buddy. Besides,
she was pretty sure he wasn't allowed to pick up a stray dog
while he was driving the company truck. The last person
who'd ever break a rule was her husband, especially in
regard to his job.

It was tempting to call George's cell phone and find out

what happened or didn't, but Vicki felt like she already knew. As much as she loved her husband, sometimes he could be so unobservant! In other words, Petie might have already been "claimed" when George arrived, and he never even noticed the sign. Besides, he was paid to pick up trash, not be on the lookout for unwanted pets. Still, it was unbelievable anyone could just tie a dog to a tree, expecting someone to pick him up—and give him a good home.

Vicki couldn't help but start crying, all for a dog she didn't even know!

Meanwhile Vicki couldn't return home quickly enough, despite no longer feeling ill. What she did feel was exhausted and depressed. Lately she'd been stressed, and everything seemed to have an over-blown effect on her.

Once she was home, Vicki left her car outside, rather than put it in the garage. Since she'd anticipated being at the clinic until dinner time, she'd planned on picking up something to eat at "Ted's." Instead, she'd order from there later and head back to town. She entered the house via the front door, avoiding passing through the utility room.

Somehow she found George's and her bed, even though it seemed like she sleepwalked from the foyer to the master bedroom.

Vicki ended up falling asleep on top of the queen-sized bed, still dressed, including her shoes.

Whatever time it was, not much time could have passed when Vicki abruptly sat up. She could have sworn there was a dog whining from the area of the garage/utility room. That was impossible, but she got out of bed anyway—and she was not pleased to notice she failed to remove her shoes. In the house she usually wore a pair of slippers or walked around in her socks.

Heading to the source of the intermittent whining, Vicki was so tired she couldn't imagine how she'd ever awakened from her nap, imagined noise or not. Meanwhile the whining became more mournful, and when she opened the utility room door, she made eye contact with a silky-coated black, white and tan dog that looked like a cross between a dachshund and a couple other breeds.

Rather than think about the sign she read earlier about a dog available for adoption, closely matching the description of the dog right before her, Vicki concluded: I'M SLEEP-WALKING. So she slammed the utility room door and went back to bed, removing her shoes beforehand this time.

What a difference it made to clear up matters. In other words, George ended up kicking himself for failing to at least attempt to get ahold of Vicki, rather than sneaking Petie into their lives. It turned out, once George explained himself (and Petie's presence), in person, she was thrilled. (He was pretty sure Vicki was mostly just relieved to find out Petie wasn't merely a figment of a sleepwalking episode.)

Petie grew on Vicki in no time at all, proving George's (ongoing) point: Working at a vet clinic had done nothing as far as helping her "move on." George never felt like it was in his place to outright tell his wife as much because she had to figure out as much on her own, and he was not even remotely a dog-person. Thanks to Petie, however, he liked to think he got a crash-course in becoming one. Most importantly, George realized he'd *wanted* to be a dog-person, but it didn't just *happen*—it had to happen *to* you.

Vicki (finally) came to her senses and decided she didn't want to work as many hours at Andover Animal Hospital. Her over-the-top dedication wasn't reflected in her paycheck. In other words she could do George a favor and be home making dinner more often than seemingly once in awhile. At the same time, she was cooking for Petie as much or more so than for her husband, yours truly. After a thorough examination of Petie by one of the veterinarians at Vicki's place of employment, it was somehow deemed necessary for the dog to receive a special diet, part of which was prepared over the stove. George refused to go so far overboard as to ask exactly what it was. Fortunately it didn't smell up the house. Despite picking up garbage for a living, he actually had a weak stomach if he smelled an aroma akin to rotting road kill. Anyway, George was proud of having rescued Petie and didn't mind at all, his wife was doting on the dog. Did that make George a bona-fide dog-person, once and for all?

It was a relief to find Vicki was happier and more relaxed than she'd been in ages. If it was thanks to a dog, at least George's theory about her had been proven correct. Obviously Petie also had a profound effect on George, which was welcomed.

The remainder of the week was uneventful. Meanwhile, George didn't return to Deb's Diner again until Friday. He usually looked forward to the weekend so he could sit around and watch TV. This weekend, however, he was anticipating putting his limited carpenter skills to use, installing "a permanent pet gate" for the utility room. Then Petie could be confined while Vicki was at work, but the door wouldn't have to be closed. That way he wouldn't have to feel "shut in." Vicki had already ordered the gate and the special hardware online and had it express-delivered. Since she was working eight until four, Petie would have to be "locked up" one more day, as she too had the weekend off.

Most likely, George would "beat Vicki home," so he'd let Petie out in the fenced yard. It would be impossible to feed him lunch because Vicki would have to cook it. Whatever she picked up for Petie at the grocery store on the way home, George hoped he was kept in mind. If nothing else, Ted's Carry-Out would do.

The parking lot of Deb's Diner was empty, typical for this time of the day. Unless several people had walked in from quaint downtown Granite, George had the restaurant to himself. He was craving his solitude more than ever today and wanted to read the paper in peace and quiet.

There was a Friday *Chicago Sun-Times* on the counter, so

Amy Kristoff

George plopped down on a stool. Looking around, he really did have the place to himself. Even the waitresses appeared to be in short supply, and he was impatient for a cup of coffee. It wasn't like he had much time to spare.

While he was waiting, George figured he might as well look at the paper. The front page had a large color picture of an interstate rest stop and the following headline to the right of the picture: "Greenwood Couple Nap While Daughter Abducted." The only reason George was curious to read on was having seen the name of a town that was right next to Andover, where Vicki and he lived.

On the next page there were separate, black-and-white, side-by-side mug shots of the distraught-looking couple, arrested for child neglect. George couldn't help staring at the wife's face. Maybe some people smiled for a mug shot when they were stoned or drunk, but she looked sober and relieved. Did she lose her mind?

"Coffee, sir?" George was asked, just as he was about to read the article about the Greenwood couple. He nodded and then looked at the waitress pouring his coffee. She was definitely new and wasn't aware he was a regular who wanted his first cup of coffee A.S.A.P. Usually he tipped generously, but he needed to really be wowed by this gal's service before doing that.

George went ahead and ordered breakfast: French toast and two scrambled eggs. In an unrelated issue, he wished he'd read her name tag, out of curiosity. She looked so young it was doubtful she'd last. She probably quit high school to take this job, assuming life was better "out here."

Finally George was able to return to the article about the Greenwood couple and their abducted daughter: Paul and Abigail Mellado were the parents of ten- year-old Andie. They had been napping in their car at a rest-stop on I-57, south of Marion, Illinois. Meanwhile, their daughter had slipped out of the backseat and was hiding from them. They were so determined she was hiding and nothing more, they searched

76

the two-way rest stop for a couple hours. Their strange behavior finally drew the attention of rest stop security. Once confronted, Mrs. Mellado broke down in tears and said her daughter was playing a cruel "hide-and-seek trick" on them. She added as an afterthought, Andie was probably upset they'd all had to leave home for good, minus their dog.

All this news was of course shocking to George. His breakfast arrived and he had barely touched his cup of coffee, a first for him. He could hardly even be bothered to make room for the waitress to place the plate of food in front of him. Not only did he forget he was starved, all he could think about was the fact a girl named Andie Mellado, who had lived with her family in nearby Greenwood, was probably dead right at this moment, all because she'd wanted to get home to her cherished dog, Petie. Meanwhile, the girl's mother and (father) was in complete denial.

George requested a fresh (hot) cup of coffee as well as the check, in case the waitress disappeared on him when he was ready to leave. He wasn't concerned about having a second cup of coffee; he wanted to get out of here as soon as possible so he could finish his work day. He couldn't wait to get home and give Petie a hug, in memory of a girl who'd truly loved her dog. And he could empathize.

Since Vicki wouldn't get home from work until a little after four, George would return home before her and could let Petie out (after giving him a hug). Because she had to cook a portion of his (Petie's) dinner, the dog would have to wait to eat. Therefore, George was in the same boat as Petie because Vicki would probably be bringing home carry-out.

Sure enough, George got home and there was Petie, patiently waiting in the utility room. He didn't tear up anything, nor did he crap or urinate on the white linoleum floor. His water bowl was dry, so he was probably thirsty as well as hungry. If his stubby tail wagging was any indication, Petie was happy as hell to see George. The hug could wait until Petie relieved himself. Trying to please a dog was obviously

a hell of a lot less complicated than trying to please a person.
With Petie back in the house and both of them hungry,
George decided there was but one thing to do until Vicki
came home: take a nap. George fell right to sleep in "his"
recliner in the den, while Petie did the same, right at his feet.

After leaving work, Vicki stopped at Ted's Carry-Out and
picked up a couple perch dinners. Then she went in the
supermarket across the street for Petie's dinner. That was all
she purchased and used the express lane to save time. Since
George was going to install a pet-gate over the weekend, Vicki
would surprise him and spend some time in the kitchen
Saturday, making dinner (following another trip to the supermarket). She was aware her husband was annoyed because
she appeared to cook for their new dog, more so than she did
for him.
Speaking of Petie, he was so good. Maybe he "knew" he'd
been saved from a horrible fate, had the "wrong" person read
the sign. Suddenly it seemed urgent for Vicki to take the
same shortcut home, she did when she originally came upon
the sign offering a free dog. A couple yanks on the sign and
it should come down. At least she hoped for as much, since
it wasn't like she had a toolbox in her car.
Vicki arrived at the property, and not only the sign but
the empty trash container were still there. She pulled the
latter right up to the tree trunk, out of the way of the road,
in case it fell over. As she was doing so, her phone rang,
which had been in her right front jeans pocket. The phone
number was the land line at home, so it had to be George.
He dove right in and said, "I fell asleep, me and Petie. Where
you at? I don't even know what time it is."
After Vicki told her husband it was a little past four-thirty, she explained where she was, what she'd been up to and
what she intended to do. Meanwhile, she couldn't help
thinking he sounded strange. Maybe it had to do with him
being disoriented from having fallen asleep.

"Don't worry about any of that, Vicki," George told her. "South Suburban will pick up the container! And I'll take down the sign this weekend, after I install Petie's new gate. Just come home!"

That did it. George sounded weird. What was going on? (!) Vicki had no idea what the answer was, but the logical course of action was to agree with him: "All right, fine. I'll see you in a few minutes. I love you."

George said he loved Vicki too, and they hung up "in unison." She felt slightly better, if temporarily.

Despite what Vicki was told about the sign, she couldn't resist pulling on it, to see if she could at least loosen it. Realizing she was unable to do so, she turned around to finally leave, only to find herself standing face-to-face with a young girl who literally looked like she'd crawled out of the bottom of a dumpster. There was a rotten smell emanating from her as well.

"Where's my dog Petie?" the disheveled girl asked, sounding angry to the point of intimidating Vicki.

Rather than reply, Vicki could only concern herself with how terrible the girl looked (and smelled), so she said, "I need to get you some help. Wait here and I'm going to leave. But I'll make sure someone comes to help you very soon." The last thing Vicki intended to do was tell this "creature" she had a phone with her. All Vicki wanted was to GET AWAY. She was terrified. If she sounded insensitive, too bad!

It felt as if the girl's eyes were burning holes in Vicki's back as she made her way to her car. She was shaking by the time she was behind the wheel and turned the ignition. It took all she had not to look in the direction of the girl before driving away. She refused to even consider calling 9-1-1 until there was at least a few hundred yards between that girl and herself. Even better, she would go home to make the phone call. It was impossible to concentrate! Was there any chance she was sleepwalking? This was a vivid experience that was more of a nightmare than a dream, should it not be "real." So was she supposed to wake herself up? What was she expected to do (to accomplish as much) when driving?

While contemplating her dilemma, Vicki started to reach for her phone, immediately becoming distracted when it seemed like it was no longer in her pocket. She happened to be driving on an especially flat stretch of road and there was no oncoming traffic, so she let herself become even more distracted by the phone's possible absence.

Then it rang. It was in her pocket, after all. Thanks to that girl, Vicki was so spooked it was impossible to think logically. Maybe never again—unless she "woke up."

Vicki nearly veered off the road while trying to extract the phone from her pocket. Immediately she slowed down, helping divert disaster. (It never even occurred to her to look in her rearview mirror before slowing her speed.) Fortunately there was no vehicle behind hers. Or there didn't seem to be.

Even though Vicki had promised herself not to talk on her phone while driving unless she could do so "safely," she went ahead and looked at the number of who was calling, and the screen read "unknown number." Vicki stared at it until realizing she was supposed to be watching where she was driving. The second she looked up, the front end of her Subaru was about to slam head-on into a utility pole. For a second she had the opportunity to wonder why her car was going so fast, as her foot was on the brake.

George abruptly leaned over his recliner's armrest and hugged Petie, who was sitting up, ears erect.

The Talking Dog

Ralph Mendell was sitting on the bed, tying his shoes, when he could have sworn a male voice said from just outside the bedroom: "Hurry up! Let's go out." It just so happened Ralph was in fact preparing to take his and his wife's mix-breed dog, Baron, out for a walk. It was entirely impossible Baron was the one who just said that, although he did suddenly appear in the doorway.

"Hey, Baron," Ralph said. "I just had a scare. Heh! I could have sworn you just told me to hurry up for our walk. What I mean is, you actually spoke words, like a person does! Ridiculous, I know. I must be hearing voices or something."

"Ralph, who are you talking to?" none other than Denise, Ralph's wife, asked him, having suddenly appeared.

A startled Ralph was standing by this time, but it'd taken forever to tie his walking shoes because the laces on the left one were knotted together.

"Hey, honey," Ralph began. "I was talking to none other than Baron. I thought I'd heard a man saying something right before Baron appeared in the doorway. It was kind of funny at the moment, so I had some fun with it." Given the way Denise looked at him, Ralph was certain he'd said something "wrong." Right away he wondered why he felt defensive in front of his wife. Maybe it had to do with the fact he loved her? He should have been flip and said, "I don't know what you're talking about, Denise." The problem was all he knew how to do was "be truthful." Was that going to be his demise?

Ralph ended up brushing past her and heading to the utility room, where Baron's leash was on a brass hook. Meanwhile, the dog was right on his heels. Obviously he had a herding breed or two in him, and he wasn't just anticipating his walk around the apartment complex. Hopefully the walk would help Ralph relax, like it usually did. As the manager of the Merrillville, Indiana "Pet World," he put in long hours and couldn't wait to get off work, except he had to return to the confines of a one-bedroom apartment. Fortunately the property manager didn't make a big deal out of the fact Baron was several pounds heavier than the stated weight limit for a dog, in the lease agreement.

Residing at "Mid-Town Apartments" was perfect for Ralph and Denise in regard to their jobs because it was within easy walking distance to work for both of them. She was employed at "Bellmer's," in "Summerset Mall," which was only a few hundred yards away. Pet World was in a free-standing building located just east of Summerset Mall. Even though he couldn't wait to get off work each day, his heart broke whenever he opened the apartment door and the first thing he laid eyes on was Baron's (eyes). All Ralph could think was, Baron looked like a dog who missed his fenced back yard. Ralph missed it too, as well as the house Denise and he owned free and clear but sold it to pay his mother's hospital, hospice, and funeral bills. Ralph was still bitter about the fact he had to do what he did; his mother, Rene, should have had plenty of money to cover everything. The problem was she'd squandered every last cent after her husband (Ralph's father, Torence), had passed away, three years before she became ill.

Ralph's marriage ended up being in jeopardy for a time, thanks to the financial sacrifice Denise and he had made for his mother. The last thing Ralph wanted to do was lose Denise because of "financial difficulties." He'd been employed by Pet World much longer than he'd been married to Denise. The point was, building (and maintaining) financial security was extremely important to him. Therefore, he didn't blame his wife for essentially freezing him out. The past few months, however, she seemed to be thawing. He liked to think he was extraordinarily patient with her and let time do the heeling. Or he meant healing. Ha! At least she hadn't stopped sleeping in the same bed with him, which was especially crucial when you had a one-bedroom apartment. Then again, what was he thinking? *He* would have been relegated to the not-so-comfortable sofa in the living room. The only good part was at least he could have left the TV on while he slept, which he liked to do (but of course didn't in the bedroom with Denise).

The only other option would have been for Ralph to leave, giving Denise her space (and hopefully doing so would have made her want him back). As it was, he was not leaving Baron behind for even a brief period of time. If (heaven forbid) Ralph and Denise divorced, there would be a custody battle involving Baron.

Ralph's and Denise's apartment was on the first floor, so there were no stairs or an elevator to bother with. Having to utilize either one necessarily made having a dog more complicated. On a day like this, he just wanted to go outside and take a walk around the spacious apartment complex. This time of the day, there were quite a few residents returning from work, but it was nonetheless rather peaceful. Some days at the store were so busy and chaotic the atmosphere became nearly unbearable. Ralph was already dreading the holiday shopping season, and the start of it was still six weeks away.

Ralph and Baron were almost finished with their loop-walk when his (Ralph's) cell phone rang. It was Denise. She was running over to "Beds and More" to use a coupon she'd just received in the mail. (Actually she was driving there, even though it was only across Route 30.) Ralph "gave his blessing" by saying he loved her and would see her when she got home. He couldn't emphasize it enough, their relationship was tenuous for awhile, and that had really scared him. Since things finally appeared to be looking up, he didn't dare open his big mouth whenever he wanted to make a comment. (What he'd *wanted* to tell Denise was, if she just stayed home, she'd save even more money than using the coupon on a nonessential item.) The dilemma consisted of the fact *he* was the one entirely at fault for their precarious financial situation—but it was technically thanks to his mother's purposefully mindless financial recklessness. Ralph never went to college, but he was naturally inclined to work hard. Meanwhile, his younger brother, Hal, was chronically unemployed (by choice). Their father only had menial jobs that barely paid the bills, yet he tirelessly worked long hours. Ralph's mother didn't work, only because her husband wanted her at home, and she was willing to be "the obedient wife," as if from another era, which it kind of was, despite not being that long ago.

Fortunately Denise always had a job, usually something having to do with cosmetics. She didn't start working at Bellmer's until the holiday shopping season last year, when she was hired as a temporary employee. Previously she'd worked at several different hair salons as a free-lance make-up artist.

One bright side to all this was Denise loved her job more than any other one she'd ever had. She never would have ended up living so close to work, except for the fact Mid-Town Apartments was the only place in the vicinity that allowed Baron to live with them. Only coincidentally was the apartment complex also close to Pet World.

With the living circumstances as of late, Denise was undoubtedly more relieved than ever to go to work. Knowing as much made Ralph feel even worse, were that possible.

Bedtime at the Mendell household was about 10 P.M. weeknights. Since this was Thursday and it was after ten, Denise and Ralph were in fact in bed. *He* was trying to fall asleep. Meanwhile, Denise was loudly flipping through a cooking-related magazine she'd purchased at Beds and More. Did she use her coupon for that or the "Orange Float" pillar candle she didn't need?

That question, along with the glare of the lamp on Denise's side of the queen-sized bed, was keeping Ralph from falling asleep. There, he admitted it. However, he was well-aware this was no time to lose his temper. Re-building Denise's and his relationship had taken a huge amount of effort for both of them, and they still had a long way to go.

Then, as Ralph was about to turn over yet again (to drop a hint to Denise, to turn off the lamp and go to sleep), he noticed (for the first time, obviously) Baron wasn't sleeping at the foot of the bed, where Ralph had assumed he'd always been. Was he underneath it?

Pretending he had been asleep but suddenly awoke, Ralph asked Denise, "Honey, are you awake?"

"Yes."

"Where's Baron?"

"He's right here."

"I admit, I never paid attention to where exactly Baron was, but I knew he was in the bedroom with us."

Denise calmly told Ralph, "Baron's always slept on my side, on a bed *you* brought back from work one day. It had a slight tear that I patched up."

Mercifully Denise finally turned off the light and went to sleep. As it was, she only cooked on the weekends, so what was the hurry, picking new recipes?

Ralph was so tense and incensed, he ended up falling immediately to sleep.

Friday morning at Pet World, Ralph could hardly wait to tell someone, seemingly anyone, about having heard his dog talk "like a person," albeit it wasn't something he could confirm. Nonetheless, he couldn't think about anything else. It was amazing he got any rest last night, given everything that was going through his head.

By eleven-thirty, Ralph couldn't take it anymore. He'd just supervised the clean-up following a fish tank mysteriously shattering in aisle one. Larry Cole was the only cashier in front, and Ralph was willing to bet money the guy's register was backed up—but Larry wouldn't dare call for help. As it was, he was due for his break.

Sure enough, there were four customers in line behind the one being served, and her credit card had just been declined. There was going to be trouble if Ralph didn't immediately put Larry on his break.

Ralph used the phone by the register to announce over the P.A., he wanted Mel (Melanie) and Toby at the registers. Then he told Larry, "Go in 'the room,' please." "The room" was essentially a bare-bones office that was directly opposite to the row of six registers. Its red-steel door had a one-way porthole window, so the occupant of the office could see out but no one could see in. That was good because Ralph was about to have a word with basement-dwelling Larry Cole. Ralph could identify with Larry's plight. The guy was only living in his parents' basement because he too had financial problems. In his case it was due to some shady investments he was "talked into." Anymore it seemed like everyone had a finance-related tale of woe.

Once Ralph helped Mel key into the register Larry was using, he was able to solve the customer's declined credit card dilemma. Meanwhile, Toby opened register number two. Finally things were moving again, so Ralph entered the office to find Larry seated in a metal folding chair, facing the doorway. The only other furniture in the room was a flimsy-looking wooden desk with another metal chair behind it.

There was only one way to handle this situation, and it involved remaining standing right in front of Larry, despite the fact he was as pale as a ghost and didn't appear to need any intimidation. Did he think he was about to get fired? Ralph was used to the guy freezing up when things got to be too much.

"You know, Larry," Ralph began, "I like your work ethic, and I can't say you do anything wrong, except you really need to ask for help when you need it. It doesn't sound like much, but under these circumstances, it's everything because customers hate waiting when they know they have to fork over their dough at the end."

While nodding (as if nervously relieved) Larry said, "Thanks, Mister Mendell, for not firing me, like I thought for sure you were going to do."

Ralph couldn't help rolling his eyes. Larry had been employed here for close to a year, and he constantly thought he was going to be fired. Obviously the guy had some issues, but who didn't? At the same time, did Larry ever listen to him? Ralph liked to think his remark about the attitude of customers was brilliant. It was the same message he was given at company meetings, except it was worded much differently. Sometimes it was hard for Ralph to keep his big mouth shut! Nonetheless, his job security depended on it, not just his work ethic.

Since Ralph had both of those taken care of, he decided Larry should be the one to hear about one suspected "talking dog." It was impossible the news would travel any farther than reclusive Larry Cole. Or so Ralph assumed. As it was, Larry Cole was probably the only guy in the whole store (including the customers at any given time) that could understand Ralph's situation as well as his mental state— other than Ralph's younger brother, Hal, worthless though *he* was.

Ralph liked to think he "did good" when he told Larry about Baron "talking." Usually Larry had 150 things to say after Ralph would finish a lecture about whatever, but on this occasion Larry was not only silent leaving "the office," he was stone-faced. Ralph even reassured him he was still owed a ten-minute break, but that comment only undid the guy even more. It was possible if Larry went outside for his break, like he usually did, he'd never return. Ralph found it hard to hold that against the guy, having unintentionally contributed to him "losing it."

As it turned out Larry did leave the store, only because the cell phone reception was better outside. He couldn't wait to call the boss of both him and Ralph, Mr. Trey Decker. At least that was what Ralph pieced together after analyzing everything that happened after giving Larry "a talking to" in the office, including having revealed TMI (too much information) regarding Baron's ability to do more than just yip and bark. He could talk like a person!

But Ralph didn't surmise this immediately. Larry got off work at 2:00, and Ralph was never so happy to see the guy depart for the day. In the meantime, Larry took every opportunity to give Ralph dirty looks. Never before had the cliché "If looks could kill" been so appropriate! Fortunately Denise didn't do that kind of thing when she was mad; otherwise Ralph would have literally gone insane.

Ralph's lunch break wasn't until 3:30 because he'd been too busy to take a break earlier. He actually liked his job the most on days like these, no matter how hectic things got. Otherwise, the work day never seemed to end.

"The office," where Ralph had met with Larry earlier, was the designated place to relax for a couple minutes and enjoy lunch. With a Taco Bell on the other side of the parking lot, it had become Ralph's favorite place to grab take-out food.

Sitting here, eating and ruminating, Ralph couldn't help thinking about "the meeting" with Larry Cole. Considering everything, it went well. Then Ralph's cell phone rang. He was tempted to ignore it, especially since it came in as an "unknown number." However, since he was still on the clock, it felt wrong to do that.

"Mendell? Are you there? Are you at work?" none other than Ralph's boss, Trey Decker, asked.

"Yes, I'm here . . . at work," Ralph answered, feeling guilty for working as much as he did, especially when confronted by his boss about the matter.

"I'm on vacation, and from what I've been told, you could use a vacation, too," Mr. Decker bellowed.

"If you don't mind, sir, could you please explain yourself?" Ralph asked his boss. More than anything he was panic-stricken about having any time off, not when he wanted to work as many hours as possible, hoping to be able to afford a house again. It was still possible Denise would decide she'd had enough of their marriage and the circumstances involving their housing situation.

In response to Ralph's question, his boss said, "I'll gladly explain myself, Mendell."

During the walk back to the apartment after work, all Ralph could think about was what Mr. Decker told him: "Larry Cole said you have a talking dog, and you were dead serious about it. You rattled him as much as you apparently already are. I know exactly what the problem is, Mendell, and it has nothing to do with your dog's potential ability to speak English. *You* need a break. We've discussed your predicament, how you want to work as much as possible to save for the down payment on a new house, but when you do what you did today, all I can say is, take the rest of the day off and the weekend too. Go home and relax and I'll see you at Pet World Monday morning at ten."

It didn't sound good. Ralph was supposed to be back at Pet World a little after eight Monday morning. Not only was he suddenly barred from arriving early, his boss was going to meet him at the door, probably to fire him. How humiliating was that, especially if Larry Cole witnessed the whole thing? Ralph was going to think long and hard about even returning to Pet World on Monday. Mr. Decker could just mail him the final paycheck. Meanwhile, Ralph would be better served to stand in line at the unemployment office.

For the time being, Ralph looked forward to seeing Baron.

Since he, Ralph, was home earlier than Denise, it would be his responsibility to feed Baron. Afterward they would go for a walk around the apartment complex. That was what Ralph enjoyed most in regard to owning a dog. Denise never had any interest in walking Baron, even when the three of them had lived in a subdivision with plenty of sidewalks. Her (limited) time with him typically consisted of kneeling to pet him for a couple minutes (at most) and then going about her business. In other words, Denise took care of Baron "out of obligation," but she had no real feelings for him. Renting a "pet-friendly" apartment didn't help matters for anyone because Denise's resentment was ingrained at this point. Their apartment was comfortable but not luxurious by any means, and Denise's job inevitably brought her in contact with plenty of gorgeous, well-off women who at least looked like they lived in nicer digs than she did.

Denise "still" looked gorgeous herself. Meanwhile, Ralph felt like stress was killing him day by day. Obviously that had culminated in him thinking Baron could suddenly talk like a person.

Wait a minute. Since Denise looked so good, was she in love? If that was the case, she was having an affair. She definitely wasn't in love with Ralph at this point. He expected that to change once they finally had a place of their own again, but that was still a ways away. He was willing to wait, but she'd evidently gotten impatient. All she needed to do was realize once and for all what a stand-up guy he really was, and she'd feel too foolish to mess around with someone on the side. Ralph preferred not to have any idea who it might be and hopefully the affair would end soon. It was absolutely heartbreaking for him!

If nothing else, Ralph intended to get out of town for a couple days, giving Denise a chance to spend some private time with her lover—and to tell him it was over.

Meanwhile, Ralph's brother, Hal, would be paid a visit shortly. Ralph didn't have to worry about infringing on the guy because he was always home and lived off a generous pension. It was no wonder he was unemployed!

As much as Ralph wanted to stay home and take care of Baron and go on plenty of walks with him, getting away for a couple days was unavoidable. Was it possible Denise would miss him, even if she had a lover? Ralph could only hope. He wished he could advise Hal on his personal life, as his brother was still heartbroken over having his wife, Linda, leave him for her boss. It was stuck in Hal's head, she was coming back. Growing up, Hal had a tendency to be obsessive. Ralph was always glad it wasn't him. Instead he was hit with sudden, "selective" insanity, which made him think Baron could talk just like a person.

Finally almost home. Ralph's walking-commute was farther than Denise's, and she often complained it was too far, especially since she was on her feet all day. Ralph was too! He never could have done it, but sometimes he wanted nothing more than to tell her to shut the f—k up. If she really wanted to drive to work so badly, go ahead! Then at least she wouldn't have to carry her high-heels in a bag and could leave her walking shoes at home.

Actually, Ralph was relieved to know Denise hadn't returned from work yet—at the expense of possibly having Baron "talk," just to mess with him while no one else was around. Despite how ridiculous it was to believe your dog was overheard speaking English, Ralph was determined he didn't imagine it. Why the hell couldn't he get that out of his head? Because he'd heard "just enough" to make him wonder? And that was the whole point. Perhaps Baron had an even more extensive vocabulary than Ralph! But Baron knew the best way to eff with Ralph, his *real* owner, was not to give away a secret: he could speak English as fluently as any human! That would be too much for Ralph to take and he'd implode. At the very least he'd take off—for good. As it was he felt like he was hanging by a thread, particularly as of late.

91

The last few steps to the building, Ralph realized he was hyper-ventilating, but it wasn't like he was completely out of shape. It was testimony to how stressed he felt, thanks to all that had happened lately—imagined or not. Then again, it was all Baron's fault. Your dog was supposed to be your best companion, your best friend!

Perhaps Denise was behind the whole charade, as in she somehow made it seem like Baron was talking, but it was her. Her cleverness couldn't have been overestimated and was what he "usually" loved about her. In this case, however, he could imagine hating her for effing with his head, in turn trying to make him hate Baron.

The apartment was on the first floor, the first door on the far southeast side of a non-descript-looking, tan brick, three-story building, one of several. Ralph had to unlock the glass door leading to the main hallway. He wasn't sure if it was bulletproof, but it appeared to be pretty thick. The point was, he shouldn't have been able to hear anything coming from Denise's and his apartment. But he did. Already Ralph was embarrassed because "someone" was in there, loudly singing—and playing a radio really loudly! Not only was Denise not much of a music lover, she was still at work. Therefore, the only occupant of the apartment could have been none other than Baron. Fortunately most of the residents on the first floor were younger couples who both worked full-time. In other words, whoever was singing probably wasn't disturbing anyone. No one else on this floor even had a dog.

In the hallway, the singing wasn't much louder, but it was more obvious than ever it was coming from Ralph's (and Denise's) apartment. It was kind of high-pitched, like it could have been Denise, but he'd honestly never before heard her sing. Besides, again, she should have still been at work. She didn't have the kind of job she could just leave early if she wanted. Or put another way: she didn't have the necessary job security because she could be easily replaced.

(Pretty, affable women weren't exactly unusual.) Ralph liked to think he comparatively had a surfeit of job security. He'd know for sure, Monday morning at ten.

Before putting the key in the lock, Ralph paused, unable to help listening to exactly what band was playing. It was Led Zeppelin, his favorite group. Although he knew the song, he couldn't recall the title. And the accompanying live singer had to be Baron.

Hair (stubble) on the back of his neck standing on end, Ralph went right back outside. He looked down and realized his hands were shaking, because he was upset more than anything (O.K., he was a little scared too). What got him was his dog was obviously having the time of his life, while *he* was hesitant to interrupt the merrymaking!

Pacing back and forth, Ralph became angry with himself for letting a *dog* dictate how his life was lived. At this point, he was only assuming Baron could actually talk like a person. There was no actual proof, as in a one-on-one with the dog—and no one else was around to pretend to "talk for him."

So what if Baron could talk? It was extremely improbable (if not entirely impossible), but perhaps he was like a parrot and could imitate a person speaking, without being aware of what he was actually saying. The problem with that theory was it didn't explain how Baron could have said, "Hurry up! Let's go out," while Ralph was tying his shoes, coincidentally doing exactly what the dog wanted.

Full of resolve, Ralph marched back into the building and prepared to unlock his apartment door, hesitating only a couple seconds while continuing to listen to the music and singing (as if there was a choice in the matter). Despite getting more and more nervous, he managed to hold his hand steady enough to unlock the door.

Just as Ralph finished turning the key, the apartment was suddenly silent. He flung the door open to find Baron sitting squat-legged about ten feet away, staring right at him, looking like he owned the place. Ralph didn't feel sorry for the dog, upon returning from work on *this* occasion.

From the bedroom, the doorway a few more feet away, Ralph heard Denise say, "Baron? Where are you? I didn't pretend I was sick and leave work early to sit around and not be entertained. Turn the music back on so we can party!"

Ralph couldn't leave fast enough. His brother had a good idea, swearing off women. And Hal had a comparatively "normal" divorce when his wife left him for her boss. Ralph didn't know *what* he was going to tell his lawyer.

The Walk to Freedom

It seemed like just another late afternoon to some people in this Phoenix neighborhood, but for Garrett Naylor, it was anything but. Again, the neighbors didn't have a clue about his situation, and it was none of their business. Garrett's main goal in life had always been to live as quietly and seamlessly as possible. Unfortunately, his wife, Cynthia, had decided to "rile him up," which was not easy to do. Honestly, he couldn't believe just how angry she'd made him. Catching her kicking his dog Merlin *and* having her deny as much sent Garrett over the edge. The good part was he took the opportunity to move on with his life—literally—and was taking his beloved Merlin with him—a thirty-pound, gray-haired mutt who looked like he was a mixture of a couple terrier breeds and a Shiba Inu. Garrett adopted him one weekend about four months ago, from a "pet rescue fair" that took place near where he worked. Bored and lonely, he went there "just to look," and he ended up with a devoted companion.

Having married Cynthia "because he got her pregnant" sounded like something a teenager would do, but Garrett was pushing fifty, and she was forty-two. Neither one had expected this to happen, but Garrett ended up being the one who was excited about the sudden change in their lives. He'd incorrectly assumed Cynthia would be grateful to him for marrying her, but she ended up treating him like shit and complained about the baby, nonstop—until her mother came over "to help," which she did about every afternoon. Cynthia wanted a full-time nanny, but that was financially out of the question. At the same time, she finally had an excuse for not having to bother looking for another job, as she was laid off shortly before realizing she was pregnant.

Garrett and Merlin were walking their way to freedom, and it was the first day of the rest of their lives! As willing as Garrett had been to dedicate himself to Cynthia and their new baby son, Duncan (her idea for a name), she wasn't interested in making the same commitment.

"Come on Merlin, why are you lagging?" Garrett asked, suspicious his devoted friend somehow "knew" they were taking a one-way walk. It was better to do this than take any more of Cynthia's insolence and total disrespect for him and his dog. She needed to be taught a lesson, and Garrett (hopefully) already did that.

It turned out Merlin had to relieve himself. "Sorry, little buddy," Garrett said. "It's just you and me now, so the last thing I can afford to do is not pay enough attention. I'm super, super, super-distracted right now. As much as I'm aware we're on a walk, I can't help but think about all that happened today, and I can't believe what I did! But what Cynthia did to you was far worse, so I have no regrets."

There was Mr. Rob Houghton, using a hose to water the colorful flowers under the dining room window of his slant-roofed, brown-brick, ranch-style house. The gorgeous landscaping gave Mr. Houghton's property its distinction, so it was no wonder he was seemingly always outside, tending to something or the other.

As lost in his tasks as Mr. Houghton could appear to be, he never failed to notice Garrett passing by with Merlin, sometimes coming over to pet the dog. On this occasion, Garrett wanted nothing more than to breeze past the guy. Because Garrett's agitation was caused by something terrible he did, it was impossible to "relax" at this time.

Just as Garrett thought perhaps he and Merlin were "safe," Mr. Houghton noticed them. "Hello! Good evening!" he called and approached them after turning off the hose.

Merlin probably looked a lot more excited to see Mr. Houghton than Garrett did. The last thing Garrett wanted to do was appear rude, but at a time like this, he honestly didn't care.

Garrett had chit-chatted with Mr. Houghton enough to find out the guy had owned dogs much of his life but didn't anymore because it was "too heartbreaking" to lose them. Also, his wife had passed away about eight years ago, and they had lived in the neighborhood since the first houses were built, almost four decades before.

Since Mr. Houghton knew "a little bit about Garrett's life," it wasn't surprising he asked how Cynthia was doing, to which Garrett replied, "She's kind of trapped right now."

"Sure, I'll bet. Having a baby is a huge adjustment for her, but she'll get used to it."

Garrett nodded. There was nothing to add. Fortunately Mr. Houghton never lingered and let Garrett go on his way. Never before had he been so relieved to be moving along. It was all too tempting to give himself away.

It seemed to take forever for Garrett and Merlin to reach Encanto Park, which was "only" three miles from home. One problem was how preoccupied he was! What was it about being mentally overloaded that made you feel physically heavier? If they really were going to walk away from home for good, it was going to take forever! Not only that, he hadn't packed a single provision for either of them. Sure, he had his wallet with some cash, a couple credit cards and a driver's license . . .

Wait. What had he been thinking? Why hadn't he grabbed some of his personal items, along with Merlin's water and food bowls (and his food), and thrown all of it in the SUV? They could have driven out of sight in no time (even though Garrett had no idea where their final destination was). It wasn't as if Merlin didn't like to ride in a vehicle.

Merlin had been a decent sport about walking this far, so he would have to keep up his good spirits to go home again.

It was getting dark by this time, and it was a bit chilly. If Merlin got too fatigued, Garrett considered carrying him. Doing so would keep both of them warm. (Garrett couldn't believe he ever thought walking away from home "for good" was a "good" idea.)

As they headed home, Garrett noticed Merlin was still full of energy, which was a huge relief. Merlin was probably relieved they were finally going back home. This was certainly the longest walk they'd ever gone on, which gave Garrett plenty of time to think.

Ever since Cynthia became Garrett's wife, she really did turn into a harridan—it wasn't an exaggeration! Why else would he have locked her up in Merlin's crate, before leaving for this "walk"? It was scary, the fury he'd felt, what it had compelled him to do!

There. Garrett admitted what he did. Truthfully, he still couldn't believe it. She couldn't either, which explained why she was too shocked to start screaming. Granted, it was a much larger crate than was necessary to keep Merlin comfortable, and Cynthia was quite petite (and short) but still. The thing of it was, Merlin never "needed" a crate for house-breaking or anything else. He was only on a leash because he could stray into traffic and get killed because he'd be following his nose.

The crate was "the beginning of the end" for Garrett and Cynthia as a couple, as she had *ordered* him to purchase it one day, not long after he'd acquired Merlin. She didn't say a word about the size it had to be, so Garrett splurged on one of the larger metal ones. Cynthia didn't dare complain about how much space the crate took up in the utility room. If she ever made a comment, Garrett planned on moving it to the bedroom – along with Merlin, of course.

Garrett and Merlin were at the corner of Indian School and 42nd Street. They had to wait for the light to change, even though no one was coming or going. He should have brought along his cell phone "just in case," but you didn't think like that when you were about to throw everything away. With a good job he was supposed to report to tomorrow . . . There was also Garrett's adorable six-month-old son, Duncan, to consider. Why hadn't he thought of his son, before? What happened to pragmatism?

All this was what Cynthia hoped Garrett would do, maybe even including locking her in Merlin's crate. No wonder she didn't say anything about how unnecessarily big it was! That seemed like a ridiculous assumption, but anything was possible at this point. No matter what, Garrett wasn't giving up his son or his dog.

A good night's sleep was what Garrett had been missing for seemingly forever. Sometimes he felt like he was dying of exhaustion, yet their son had nothing to do with it, as he'd been sleeping through the night just fine. Maybe that would change, but Duncan appeared to be just like Merlin: neither one wanted to cause a fuss. (Garrett couldn't resist getting in another dig at the ridiculousness of making the dog suddenly have to spend most of his time in a humiliating, confining crate.)

Cynthia was jealous of Merlin—that was the problem! It had nothing to do with an irrational fear regarding Merlin, attacking Duncan in his crib. First of all, Merlin was completely indifferent to the baby, and he was too small to reach the kid anyway. And that was where Duncan had been spending most of his time because he slept so much and his mother didn't care to bother holding him. Cynthia never was one to dote much or be affectionate, but having Duncan only made her less so, of all things—especially toward her newborn baby!

Garrett's mother, Helene, was well-apprised of "the situation" involving Cynthia and her overall lack of interest in Duncan, and she was more than happy "to step in if need be." However, Cynthia's mother, Joan, knew what was going on too, and her presence took precedence. Not to be pessimistic, but Cynthia's mother was going to be sorry for catering to her 42- year-old daughter as liberally as she did. A day of reckoning had to be near.

Not to be making excuses, but Garrett had a terrible day at work, and things seemed to disintegrate from there. He didn't have a hugely stressful job per se, but he did have to deal with a lot of employees who wore his patience thin by the end of each work day. Garrett really had enough, but he'd never kick anything, except maybe the kitchen door. He didn't have it in him to be curt with Cynthia, even if she was seriously pissing him off. Perhaps his anger and frustration had been bottled up longer and more intensely than he'd had any idea. Obviously there was only so much he could take, especially when given "a push," via witnessing Cynthia kicking Merlin.

Garrett still couldn't believe he'd married a b— with a capital "B". And to have her deny she actually kicked Merlin! That only made Garrett look stupid, maybe because he was the one with a conscience.

There had been no recourse but to shove Cynthia into the crate. It had been his "last word" with her, and he was proud of himself for "letting his actions do the talking." The two of them had already had too many profanity-laced screaming matches, particularly after he'd brought Merlin home.

From the beginning of their relationship, the whole problem had been Cynthia's overall aloofness, despite Garrett's efforts to become close to her. He felt like he never really knew her, and she didn't want him to. Nonetheless, he found her likable, and she was a super cook (when she *felt like* cooking). Acquiring Merlin was Garrett's escape from going insane with loneliness—even while being married *and* having a newborn!

Cynthia became even more cold toward Garrett once her pregnancy was noticeable. She claimed to feel "too fat to be pretty," yet she looked better than she ever had, including the "added weight." By the time she had Duncan, Garrett had had enough of what had turned into total insolence from her. She had to have been at least somewhat aware of what her negative attitude was doing to Garrett. Rather than be incensed he adopted a dog, she should have been relieved he didn't "splurge" and have a love affair. To her, Garrett's devotion to his dog was probably worse/ more unacceptable. Cynthia grew up without any pets to care for, while Garrett's family always had one or two dogs. One of them was typically a stray, as the Naylor family's property only consisted of a few acres but was on a rather remote country road in south-western Ohio. It happened to be a popular spot to dump unwanted dogs. Perhaps dumping cats wasn't the thing to do because their place wasn't a working farm (but it was surrounded by thousands of acres of cropland).

The "good part" about Garrett's day at work was he'd been able to leave almost forty minutes sooner than usual. Obviously Cynthia hadn't expected to have him walk in on her while she was kicking Merlin and saying something loudly but was completely incoherent. It didn't help, Merlin was yelping for mercy, drowning out Cynthia. Merlin wasn't in his crate only because she must have pulled him out of it—so she could kick him. Merlin then attempted to flee the unwarranted punishment and ended up by the back door, where he proceeded to urinate on the floor while watching Cynthia come after him.

Meanwhile, Garrett had witnessed the whole scenario while standing in the foyer, frozen with disbelief. Evidently Cynthia didn't hear him enter via the front door, versus the door leading from the two-car garage to the kitchen and utility room.

Much to Cynthia's surprise (and dismay), Garrett finally came to his dog's rescue. Her initial expression was absolutely priceless. It gave him added impetus to shove her into the crate, exactly where she belonged, for a variety of reasons.

101

Garrett's heart swelled with pride, thinking about how protective he was of his dog. It proved how he'd be for Duncan, should the need arise (despite the fact he temporarily forgot about his kid, upon embarking on this walking-adventure).

Not to continue making excuses about everything, but Cynthia's ongoing negative attitude apparently consumed all his mental energy. He really did love her and wanted her to be HAPPY! Of course that was impossible, so when enough was enough, why not shove her in Merlin's crate? (Garrett still couldn't believe he actually did it.) He still didn't feel the least bit repentant, which was a relief in one way but also puzzling.

Merlin finally appeared to be getting weary, so a break was in order. It was almost dark by this time, and it would be getting more and more chilly. Unfortunately Garrett was too tired to come through and carry the dog, as he'd previously considered doing. Cynthia would just have to wait for Garrett to "rescue" her. He'd do that after he'd laid down some new rules for their life together, starting with her talking to him as if he were a person and not a dog. Garrett talked to Merlin like *he* was a person!

Most likely, however, Cynthia's mother would be the one to save her daughter—which was actually more appropriate because Joan had never failed to step in and save her. For that alone, Joan needed to be taught a lesson, so maybe catering to her forty-something kid would be its own reward someday, in the worst way.

Once Joan Mahl's daughter married "that guy Garrett who was a dog lover," Joan just knew the day would finally come when poor Cynthia would snap. Who could blame her? *He* got her pregnant, not that Cynthia didn't deserve her share of "the blame." However, she probably got talked into not taking any precautionary measures, simultaneously assuming she was "too old to worry about the issue." Joan knew her daughter wasn't great mommy material. The good part was Joan absolutely loved being a grandmother and was more than happy to help. As reluctant as Joan was to admit it, Garrett had really stepped up as a dad and appeared to enjoy the experience—unlike Cynthia. It was very disappointing to witness as much on a daily basis.

Nonetheless, Joan wouldn't let herself get depressed about the issue. She enjoyed her grandson Duncan's company too much. It helped give her incentive when showing up at Cynthia's (and Garrett's) house in the afternoon, only to be met with indifference by Cynthia. Since Joan took Duncan off her hands for an hour or two, sometimes more, that was the last reaction that should have been expected. Sometimes Cynthia was taking a nap when Joan showed up, making it necessary for Joan to let herself in. Duncan would be in his crib, near his mother. Usually he was awake but never cried. Thank God because there was no telling what Cynthia would have done if he did start making noise. For one, she'd move him to "his future room," next door. She'd already banished Garrett's stupid dog to a crate in the utility room. Good for her, in that regard at least.

On this particular afternoon, Joan was running later than usual because her hair stylist had had a family emergency and pushed her appointments back. It was already after four, and Joan was usually at Cynthia's by 3:45, so she called her on her cell phone to let her know she was on her way. There was no answer, so Joan left a message, even though Cynthia was probably taking a nap. This way, Joan had a head's up regarding letting herself in. It really was unfair, how mean Cynthia could be when she realized her mother had let herself in the house and was taking care of Duncan (provided he was awake). Otherwise, Joan would tidy up the house as much as possible, without making too much noise.

The first thing Joan noticed upon reaching Cynthia's (and Garrett's) house was his SUV was in the driveway. Even though he had become "family" by marrying Joan's daughter, she honestly couldn't stand him. Typically he didn't return home from work until a little later, and the first thing he did was take that dumb dog of his outside. Sometimes he even took it for a walk, having barely greeted Cynthia. Admittedly, she could be kind of unfriendly, but she deserved more effort than that from her own husband!

Stepping in the house, something immediately didn't seem right. Joan wanted to leave but was compelled to remain, if only to make sure her grandson was O.K. There. She admitted it; she wasn't even half as concerned about the welfare of her daughter and son-in-law. Sometimes it was difficult to even care about Cynthia, she could be such a b**ch! As for Garrett, Joan already beat up on him enough. It wasn't his fault he was a total fool.

Glancing in the master bedroom, apparently Duncan was in his crib, fast asleep. Meanwhile, his mother wasn't in bed, so that had to mean Cynthia left her kid there, with the assumption he would remain asleep while she and Garrett took his dirty, smelly dog for a walk. Cynthia was probably "forced" to satisfy a demand of her husband's by accompanying him. Joan had already dropped several hints, Cynthia needed to get her butt back to work and do *something* to earn even a little income so she wasn't so entirely dependent on her husband. It was hard for Cynthia because she could be so lazy, which Joan might have already mentioned, but it couldn't be emphasized enough. Cynthia didn't get that from either of her parents, so some of that laziness was from having been spoiled. Joan deserved the blame for that one, and her husband Wendell had warned her about what was being done to their only child, when Cynthia was growing up.

Just as Joan turned to leave, figuring it was just as well to let her grandson keep sleeping, she heard a whimper from the utility room, at the far end of the house. That was where the dog's crate was. What was that thing's name again? Morton? Mervin? Merlin? Yes, that was it.

Then there was another whimper and another after that. The more Joan heard, the less it sounded like it was from a dog and the more it sounded like it was from a person. She hurried to the utility room, and that was the last thing she remembered.

Garrett (and Merlin) really did walk far! Finally, however, they were almost home. Merlin still wasn't lagging, but Garrett was. The good part was he could see his SUV, albeit way down the street. Behind it was his mother-in-law's car. Fortunately she always parked it far enough behind his vehicle, he could back around it if need be. She never parked next to his vehicle because Cynthia inevitably took off someplace while there was free babysitting for Duncan.

"Just a few hundred more yards, Merlin, and we'll be home," Garrett said, reassuring himself more than anyone else. Nonetheless, Merlin had been a real trouper.

Almost home, Garrett nearly started to cry, he was so relieved. Even Merlin got in on the celebrating and started wagging his corkscrew tail as well as pulling on the leash, despite the fact he had to be exhausted. At least he didn't have to deal with anyone's wrath once they went inside. Meanwhile, who knew what Garrett's mother-in-law would say to him for having locked her wonderful daughter in Merlin's oversized crate? Garrett figured Cynthia would have one word for him: Divorce.

After entering the house via the front door, Garrett let Merlin loose, only to hear him start barking from the utility room, where his crate was located. All Garrett could think was, *Come on, what now? There's no way Cynthia's still in there, not with her mother having shown up to rescue her before me.*

Garrett checked Duncan's crib and there he was, awake and looking ready to start bawling. Something was definitely amiss. Then Garrett sprinted to the utility room to find Merlin barking at a silent, motionless Joan, who was somehow stuffed into Merlin's crate. That was a feat because she was quite a bit taller and a lot heavier than her daughter. Meanwhile, Cynthia was nowhere to be seen.

After confirming Cynthia's car wasn't in the garage, Garrett grabbed the still-barking Merlin by the collar and told him, "We're out of here, whether Cynthia's mom is alive or dead. I have nothing to do with what her daughter did to her. We're grabbing the baby and driving this time around."

His Number Is Up

The following was an excerpt from the June issue of *Man World* magazine and the title of the "humorous" article was "Blast-Off or Be Cast-Off, Loser!":

Yes, you know that kind of woman. You've dated too many of them by now. They aren't half-bad to know, but put them behind the wheel of an automobile and you'd never recognize them, not in the physical sense. Lips pursed, eyes riveted on the road, one lane or three, they'll drive in all three simultaneously. They don't wait, especially not for sex. Your member isn't in proper working order when they want it, and you're the one who's screwed. You might as well take a number and go stand in line. They'll find someone else because it's all in the timing and yours is way off. Face it, you're no more useful than a piece of furniture their over-stuffed apartments don't need. They all claim to be in desperate search for 'The Perfect Man,' but they fail to realize they have a few faults of their own. You, mean-while, would die for them . . .

Brandon Burr was reading this while seated on the bus stop bench at the corner of Thomas Road and 52nd Street in Phoenix, Arizona. Even though he couldn't help chuckling, the contents of the article rang all too true. As it was, reading was a good distraction from all the annoying traffic whizzing past. Just because it was morning rush-hour, did

107

people really need to hurry so fast?

Lately it seemed like everything bothered him, and some of that had to do with the fact he hadn't been getting enough sleep, thanks to his new apartment. Actually, it was mostly thanks to more than one neighbor's dog that barked seemingly nonstop. The three-story, tan adobe building where his studio apartment was located, was across the street from an older subdivision whose bungalows had more fenced back yards than in-ground pools, hence the abundance of canines. The extent of Brandon's familiarity with dogs consisted of what his ex-girlfriend's Pembroke Welsh Corgi did to him, which was to make him feel as unwelcome as possible at her apartment. Caroline and Brandon barely dated before he moved in because she didn't like to be alone (and the lease on his overpriced place was up).

Before it was all over, Brandon managed to get fired, which in turn caused him to get behind on the payments for his silver 2012 VW Beetle Turbo. That was particularly crushing because it was only thanks to his car, he'd met Caroline. Then again, what was he saying? Overall she'd made him more miserable than happy, if only because it was almost impossible for *her* to be happy.

Unfortunately, Brandon's new job didn't pay as well as the old one, and the commute was longer. As it was, since he'd deservedly lost his job, it wasn't easy finding another good job. Because he could no longer afford a car, riding the bus gave him plenty of time to do some reading. Obviously he could also read while waiting for the damned bus, but he wasn't complaining. He had way too much to be grateful for! (And he could be extremely sarcastic.)

Occasionally, on his way to work (at his former job), Brandon would stop at a quick mart for a cup of coffee and a doughnut. There were a couple different ones he passed, and he typically stopped at the first one if it wasn't too busy or proceeded to the next one. Usually he wasn't much for having anything in the morning, but sometimes he was too hungry to wait for lunch.

One day, Brandon had his morning craving and was about to pass the first quick mart option because it was too busy, when he noticed a leggy brunette exit a red Beetle! It was possibly even a turbo. He had to find out. Fortunately the guy on a motorcycle, parked to her right, was just leaving. Brandon could park his Beetle next to hers, and he soon confirmed it was indeed a turbo. It even had a sunroof like his! He felt like he was destined to meet his soul mate at some point because he was such a decent, patient, well-intentioned guy. It was hard not to feel like he'd been taken for granted by one too many (ex-)girlfriends, and his number was finally up. Brandon didn't find a girl to live with by the end of the year (it was early March) he would quit livi— quit women. Instead, he'd get a dog, even though he would readily admit to having no desire to do so, if only because he'd never been around one and frankly detested them.

The line at the register was long, and she was right ahead of Brandon after he'd gotten his coffee and a glazed doughnut. She briefly turned around, and he couldn't resist asking her, "How do you like your Beetle? I have a silver one too, a turbo, also with a sunroof. It's an automatic."

She smiled, which made her even prettier. Then she told Brandon, "I like mine a lot, but it's a stick. I'm often asked how I can stand driving one with all the traffic around here, but I like it. It gives me something to do."

Brandon laughed, as she sounded adorable when she made that last comment, although he did make note of the overly-intense look in her big brown eyes. Nonetheless, he let it pass, not holding it against her she was probably one of those terror-behind-the-wheel women. They weren't as easy to keep happy as one would think, but he didn't yet know this and had yet to read the article in *Man World*. That beautiful smile of hers couldn't be ignored, and she flirted with him without appearing to be doing so. Damned if Brandon didn't feel like he was falling in love right there in line at

"Super-Quick" quick mart.

As much as Brandon wanted to introduce himself to this beautiful woman, he refused to be pushy and would let fate take its course. The truth of the matter was he was desperate to get to know her. She was way above average in the looks department and was undoubtedly accustomed to having males try to get noticed by her. He was beyond thrilled she didn't reply, "So what?" when he'd told her he had a VW Beetle like hers. That would have been a fate worse than death.

The dilemma with Brandon was he wanted to settle down and get married. He imagined kids in the picture at some point, although he was barely thirty, which was considered "young" anymore. He sure didn't feel young, if only because of knowing what he wanted. The biggest problem was finding a woman in the 25-30 age range who felt the same way.

It turned out she was empty-handed while standing in line because she needed a pack of cigarettes (but she was trying to quit and would succeed). Brandon hadn't even thought about what she might have been purchasing because he was so stuck on *her.* Usually he was very turned-off by women who smoked.

Brandon had to wait but a week before he ran into Caroline again. This time it was at none other than the service/parts department of "Mountain View VW" at the corner of McDowell Road and 68th Street. He'd stopped in to buy some touch-up paint (a silly mistake on his part caused the necessity of that), while she just paid for an oil-change.

Having exchanged hellos with her, Brandon couldn't resist outright asking her, "Do you work far away from here?" meaning, how did she manage to do without her car, unless a *boyfriend* was in the picture, to give her a ride?

Again, she had the opportunity of giving him a snotty reply, but she instead told him, "Actually, 'Super-Quick,' where we first talked, was like a halfway point east and west between work and home, and this place is totally out of the way, but I had the day off. But that's not to say I have loads of free time. I've had my share of fourteen hour days to make up for it. And I'm like the guinea pig of 'Fit Female Fitness.' Mostly I answer the phone and handle day-to-day stuff, but my hours are erratic because I'm always covering for the gals that have kids and husbands."

She was so endearing and was being so open with Brandon, it felt like the whole meeting was a dream. Nonetheless he came to his senses and told her, "Don't feel bad. I'm the company scapegoat."

The way she laughed in response and then smiled, really did Brandon in. Then she said, "I seriously doubt it."

Brandon couldn't help gloating, certain he'd scored at least two points: one for having made her laugh and one for making her believe he was a real man, rather than just another loser. However, he still had no idea what her "boyfriend-status" was, but he hardly cared. He was having way too much fun chatting with her and had long ago forgotten about purchasing the touch-up paint.

It seemed acceptable at this point to ask her what her first name was, but she first proceeded to ask him, "Where do you work?"

"'Messing, Limited.'"

"I know Sandy," she said, sounding as if the two were at the very least, close acquaintances. Sandy Messing was locally renowned because she inherited her philanthropic father's printing company, and although some said she was a great businesswoman, others rolled their eyes and said it was only a matter of time until she ran the business into the ground. Unfortunately she could afford to do just that and walk away. Some undoubtedly hated her for it. Brandon sure as hell did. What he'd give to sit in her chair and pretend to be "the boss," if only for a few minutes. She never locked her office door because she knew everyone was too afraid of her to dare snoop (or anything else).

As if reading Brandon's mind, she said, "*My* boss is a total bitch. I'd leave if I could, but I can't complain about the pay. And I'm used to the crazy hours. How can I complain when I can get stuff like this done and still have time to go home and play with my dog?"

O.K. Brandon knew she smoked (having witnessed what she'd been waiting in line for at the quick mart), and now he knew she had a dog. Nevertheless, he ploughed ahead.

Brandon didn't think he was being too intrusive by introducing himself by this time. In turn he hoped she'd do the same—and she did. Her name was Caroline Vaca and she made the suggestion they get together "sometime." He about fainted when hearing her say that. All he could think was she liked him, too.

The ultimate proof Caroline had an interest in him? She gave him her phone number! He eagerly took it, never thinking to ask her if she was dating anyone. Nor did he give her *his* number, figuring it more gentlemanly not doing so.

Before departing, Caroline said, "I'm taking advantage of the rest of my day off and going home to take my dog Tippy for a walk. Even though I work for a fitness-oriented place, I spend most of my time on my butt, which is how I started smoking."

Brandon told her it was "nice to meet her" (which wasn't the half of it). He brushed off the fact her dog was obviously a big part of her life. It couldn't have been said he wasn't warned.

Naturally Brandon neglected purchasing the touch-up paint. He'd scratched his Beetle the very day he drove it home from the dealership, which was already several months ago. Realistically, did it even matter at this point? All he cared about was going home and calling Caroline, to ask her out on a date. Of course he couldn't do that because he'd decided it was necessary to wait "at least a week," determined his patience would impress her. Plus, she would think he was super-busy, which always seemed to impress women, if only because *they* were typically so busy, themselves.

Once a week had finally passed, rather than be excited about contacting Caroline, Brandon was a nervous wreck. It had to do with asking her whether she was seeing anyone. All he wanted was the truth. If she was into dating more than one guy, he could tolerate the situation up to a point. (He didn't intend to get serious with her and then have her dump him for someone else she'd been seeing even before him.)

Figuring Caroline wasn't busy about 5:30 P.M. on Monday, Brandon called her but there was no answer. He decided to try her mobile phone a couple more times before leaving a message—which he proceeded to do around 7:40. Doing so was difficult when he suspected she might be blowing him off. He reminded himself it was far less devastating for that to happen than to have her dump him later on. Therefore, he left his call back number in case it wasn't on her phone. He was positively tortured about whether he'd appear condescending and redundant for having done that. Hopefully there would be an opportunity to show her how earnest he was.

Just as Brandon was about to give up and go to bed, as it was close to eleven, Caroline finally called. Sounding out of breath, she explained she'd been at an 'emergency animal clinic,' as her dog, Tippy, had eaten a portion of one of her slippers, in turn becoming ill. The dog's misbehavior had been explained away by Caroline saying, "She does things like that when she's mad at me. She probably didn't like the fact I was called in to work later in the day when *she* assumed I had the whole day off, like last Monday."

The warning bells about this woman were blaring in Brandon's ears, yet he was apparently suddenly deaf. Maybe the decibel level of the warning bells did it.

As desperately as Brandon wanted to ask Caroline if she

was seeing anyone, he went ahead and asked her out to dinner. If she accepted, he figured she wasn't *too* tied down.

"Yes, I'd like to go out with you," she readily replied. "Where do you want to meet?"

When Brandon recommended "Lido's" and heard her gasp, he wished he could have seen her expression. Although the restaurant had excellent food, you didn't go there unless you had money to spend. Once Brandon took care of his rent and car payment(s), there wasn't a lot left over, but this was definitely a special occasion, the first date with the woman he wanted more than anything to make his wife.

Caroline was the one who proceeded to suggest the following evening for meeting at Lido's. Brandon was thrilled by her enthusiasm, but he wanted a second to absorb all this. He wanted her to remember/realize *she* was the one pushing for moving things along so quickly. At the same time, he wanted nothing more than to keep up.

It appeared (for the time being at least) there was nothing to worry about. The dinner was a total success, if Brandon did say so, himself. Caroline was easy to converse with, as in she willingly made plenty of small talk but never mentioned her dog, even once.

Seriously, was it really so awful Caroline had a dog and dearly loved it? She looked stunning when she met Brandon in the white brick entryway of Lido's, the colorful abstract paintings on the walls, the perfect backdrop. This was the first time he'd seen her "dressed up," and he could hardly keep from ogling her. It looked like she'd pulled out all the stops: long, loose, wavy brown hair; a made-up face; and colorful chandelier earrings. Her outfit consisted of a sleeveless, deep purple blouse with a frilly collar and a black, above-the-knee pencil skirt with a wide turquoise "V" on the front. Her high-heeled black sandals appeared to make her taller than him by an inch or two. What really got to Brandon was Caroline's eyes no longer had that wild-eyed look.

Maybe the mascara, eyeliner and shadow offset her beady brown eyes, was all.

The car valet eliminated the opportunity for Brandon to be chivalrous and walk Caroline to her car. Instead he'd give the valet five bucks to cover both of their cars—and hopefully she'd notice and think it was all for hers. As it was, there was no final opportunity for privacy, other than when the valet briefly disappeared to retrieve her car. It was just as well because Brandon needed to make sure he didn't move too fast.

Brandon's car was gone, his well-paying job was gone, his "dream" girlfriend/future wife was gone . . . At this point he would have been ecstatic to see Tippy run up and jump on his lap. The second best option was the arrival of the bus he'd been waiting for seemingly forever.

When Caroline told Brandon she wanted to see him again, he was elated, of all things. Also, he could hardly wait to make sure she had his phone number. At first it seemed like they were a reasonably compatible couple. Tippy must have noticed that too and made sure to derail them. That damned dog wanted Caroline all to herself. Worse, Caroline did nothing to prevent as much and even appeared to enjoy the competition for her attention and affection. The thing of it was, Tippy initially acted indifferent toward him before "deciding" she'd had enough of Brandon's close relationship with Caroline. As it turned out, the dog needn't have "worried" so much; her owner found a replacement for Brandon without any trouble at all, and that was what had forced him to be uprooted. And he'd loved Caroline, even though he hadn't yet felt like it was time to tell her. She certainly hadn't said it to him (which "said it all").

It was imperative Brandon keep reminding himself to move on—otherwise he'd wallow in self-pity and wouldn't last much longer.

Amy Kristoff

Barely had Brandon awakened in the A.M. and had to get ready for work when his phone "rang" (it was actually still on vibrate). He wanted to ignore it but the caller was Caroline! He was so excited and nervous he could hardly answer. However, he managed to do so and after greeting her, she said, "I hope I didn't wake you, Brandon."

"No, no. I had to get up anyway."

"I wanted to thank you again for dinner last evening. I had a tremendous time. As I mentioned before, I'd like to see you again. I thought maybe . . ."

Brandon (almost) rudely cut Caroline off to offer this invite: "I would like you to be my guest at my place for dinner tonight."

Not surprisingly Caroline laughed, so he felt it was necessary to reassure her by saying, "I'm a graphic artist for my livelihood, but I actually went to culinary school intending to be a chef, so I'd like to demonstrate my skills. I promise to be a gentleman."

Since she abruptly quit laughing, initially Brandon thought maybe he'd offended her by sounding so boastful. Instead she asked what time it would be O.K. to come over, even sounding meek, of all things.

Brandon impressed Caroline with his culinary skills. (He served Cornish hen with wild rice.) She not only made a pig of herself (her own description), she drank almost a whole bottle of sparkling wine. Brandon barely drank a glass, as he wasn't much of a drinker. She must not have been either because she passed out on the living room sofa while he was putting the dishes in the dishwasher. He'd only left her alone for a couple minutes! As it was, she'd told him to take care of that task and she'd wait.

Being a gentleman, Brandon only removed Caroline's shoes and carefully positioned her on the sofa so that she was comfortably laying down. Then he retrieved a blanket from the closet and placed it over her before returning to the kitchen to finish cleaning up.

116

Caroline was still passed out when Brandon came back to the living room, so he couldn't resist turning on the TV and going through the channels (standing the whole time). It was impossible for him to relax when his date was unconscious on the sofa!

Fortunately Caroline came to after about thirty minutes, about the time Brandon had enough standing and finally wanted to relax a little. She abruptly sat up and looked around, pushing the yellow cotton blanket off as she said, "I have to get home and let Tippy out. I'm so sorry I fell asleep or whatever I just did. I can't believe it. I'm embarrassed." Then she stood up, only to teeter so much she almost fell back on the sofa. Brandon tried to help steady her, but she waved him away. Instead he retrieved her shoes. She managed to put them back on, despite her condition. However, she didn't say a word about why they weren't still on her feet, so Brandon didn't say anything either.

Obviously Caroline intended to drive herself home, so Brandon watched her make her way to the front door, vowing to stop her if she wobbled even once. Not only did she look fine, she didn't even bother saying good-bye! Maybe she wanted to get home and have a cigarette, having announced upon her arrival she'd just managed to quit smoking.

The next morning Caroline instantly redeemed herself by leaving a message on his phone while he was taking a shower before work: "Brandon, it's Caroline. I wanted to know if you'd like to come to my place this evening around six-thirty? I'm not a trained chef like you, but my mother and grandmother gave me a few cooking lessons here and there, and I think my creations are pretty tasty. Anyway, let me know if you can come so I can pick up some things on my way home from work. Just call or text me and I can give you directions. Bye."

Brandon listened to this message with a towel wrapped around his waist. (He was relatively modest even when he was alone.) Once he was finished it felt like he needed another shower. It did him in just knowing Caroline was interested in him. He'd already been dreading the possibility their relationship would start out too one-sided for her to catch up.

Even though Brandon wanted to call Caroline right back, he decided it would "look better" if he waited until he got to work. Wouldn't that help keep him from appearing too eager?

Still waiting for the bus. Brandon felt like he'd spent his whole life doing this and nothing else. It sure seemed like there was more traffic than ever this morning. Then again, it was two hours later than the time he had been waiting when he was first hired for this current job. The hours were abruptly cut when an issue arose regarding health insurance for "newer" employees like himself. It'd been impossible to find a job even remotely close to what he formerly did. What didn't help matters was the fact he was technically "fired" from his former job. Brandon didn't have it in him to fight the issue. He was distracted by the fact Caroline, in the meantime, "fell in love at first sight" with his boss's son. Before that even happened, Brandon had already become accustomed to sharing the rent and wondered how he'd managed on his own, if only the mental aspect of it. Granted, Caroline's apartment was pricier (and roomier) than his was, but neither one was exactly a bargain. Now he was renting a comparative dump, and it was still nearly unaffordable. He sure as hell wouldn't be able to invite anyone to dinner. It was what he got for splurging on a dinner or two out with Caroline, assuming all along she was going to fall in love with him and eventually marry him (once he proposed).

After Brandon had dinner at Caroline's, they spent some time sitting around talking. And yes, she was a decent cook. It was the first occasion on which he'd seen her completely relaxed without being unconscious. Tippy ignored them to the point she slept on her bed by the washer and dryer the entire time Brandon was there. The apartment didn't have an actual utility room, so the full-sized appliances were in an alcove next to the kitchen, across from a half-bath. Brandon would have killed to have had even a stack-unit washer and dryer in his apartment, versus having to share the use of a full-sized washer and dryer.

Although Tippy didn't think much of Brandon's visit that evening, Caroline did and asked him to spend the night—so he did.

When Caroline asked him the next morning if he wanted to move in with her, of course he said yes. It seemed too good to be true his lease also happened to be up and he wanted to move anyway. Not only was he sick of living alone, he wanted nothing more than to live with the very woman he wanted to make his wife.

Some would have said they "moved too fast," so no wonder Brandon and Caroline's relationship didn't last. At least they (or mostly *he*) tried. Looking back (obsessing over every single facet of their time together), Brandon concluded Caroline wasn't nearly as committal as he was, which was fine, it was her prerogative. What angered him was she *acted* like she was one-hundred-percent into making the relationship work.

Fortunately Brandon had the sense to put the majority of his possessions in a storage unit until he was "sure" Caroline and he were "the real thing." He knew what *he* felt, but could he be sure she'd ever catch up? It was just as well he never ended up telling her he loved her. His descent would have only ended up being even more painful.

Having moved in with Caroline (and Tippy), Brandon only wanted to fit in and not disrupt anything. So, that first night, when he had to use the bathroom after everyone had gone to bed, he didn't dare turn on any lights. It was dark as hell in the bedroom, but since he knew the general direc-

Amy Kristoff

tion of the bathroom, he figured there wouldn't be a problem. So intent was he on staring at the dim outline of the bathroom doorway, he paid no heed to what might be underfoot, not that he could have seen the long, hollowed-out chew bone. Not only did he hurt his bare right foot by stepping on the thing, he ended up tripping. Grabbing the bathroom doorframe was all he could do to break his fall slightly. At least he located his destination. In the meantime, he must have yowled because Caroline abruptly sat up and turned on the lamp by her side of the bed, exclaiming, "What was that?"

"Nothing. Just me," Brandon replied, attempting to make light of the situation, even though he wanted to scream because of the pain coming from several different parts of his body.

"Brandon, what are you doing on the floor?" Caroline then asked him. After he explained what happened, she said, "I'm sorry," before turning off the lamp and going back to sleep, just like that!

Brandon was "floored," and he wasn't trying to make a joke. Although he hadn't expected Caroline to leap out of bed and help him, it seemed like there was something more she could have done.

The following morning Brandon almost overslept. He didn't have to report to work at an exact time, but 8:30 was his goal. When living alone there was never a problem with him being late, nor was there a need to set his alarm clock. Having spent the first night with Caroline, he was exhausted, O.K.? No, he wasn't referring to hours of passionate sex. Rather, after he finally made it back to bed, he couldn't fall sleep. It didn't help he was in pain, but he was also suffering from insomnia, a rarity for him.

Realizing he'd neglected to pick up some more disposable razors, Brandon borrowed one of Caroline's. Either because he was exhausted, in a hurry, or was using a "woman's razor," he managed to nick himself pretty good between his nose and upper lip. After dabbing it with a towel several dozen times, it finally (almost) stopped bleeding. The only way he could proceed with getting dressed and getting on with the day was if he put an adhesive strip on the cut, as goofy as he probably looked (and felt).

In the meantime, Caroline had offered to make Brandon some toast and a couple scrambled eggs. Terrific! He was starved. It'd been a long time since anyone cooked him breakfast. He didn't have to go as far back as when he was in college and would return home between semesters, but it was close. Brandon's thing was, he didn't feel like it was "worth it" to move in with a girl unless he "felt something" for her. He sure felt it for Caroline, but it was necessary he keep his cool, give her plenty of time to "catch up."

By the time Brandon finally sat down to eat, Tippy had positioned herself to his far left and was already intently watching him. All Brandon wanted was to have his breakfast in peace, albeit he was aware that having an animal staring at him was technically a non-issue. He should have only been concentrating on eating, as Caroline had prepared above-average scrambled eggs, and she even "toasted the toast" just right. The coffee was perfect as well. Was love compelling him to declare this?

The way to Caroline's heart was Tippy. The dilemma consisted of the fact the mere sight of the thirty-five-pound ball of fur made him want to kill it by throttling its short, thick neck. And having the thing watch him eat was definitely "overkill," for want of a better word. That dog's piercing brown eyes looked like a human's!

With a slice of plain toast on a napkin, Caroline sidled over to the table to join Brandon. Looking fresh-faced and stunning, she was wearing a floor-length, aqua-colored terrycloth robe, her hair piled atop her head. Brandon not only stopped eating but forgot about Tippy for a few seconds.

Before sitting across from Brandon, Caroline asked, "What's that above your lip?" to which he briefly explained

121

what had happened, only to have her literally start to cackle, going on and on. It was the most annoying sound he'd ever heard. He just wanted it to end.

Once Brandon was at work he was O.K with being there, but he sure didn't miss anything about it when he left. It didn't help, his boss' moods were so unpredictable. There were ongoing rumors she had a major drinking problem, so maybe her moodiness was an indication of her constantly recovering from a hangover.

Having to show up with the adhesive strip above his upper lip should have been a total non-issue for Brandon, given the fact everyone was an adult employed here at Tip-Top Printing. His only concern was none other than Sandy Messing, his boss.

Indeed, no one said a word about the adhesive strip, including Allen Munro, who was prone to making wisecracks about the stupidest, most inane things. However, Allen had been pretty distracted lately, so it wasn't too surprising he didn't notice.

Since Sandy didn't usually show up until ten-thirty or even eleven, the verdict was still out on her reaction, if any, to his appearance. Again, it all depended on her mood. He was in no hurry whatsoever to find out. Maybe he'd "get lucky," and she wouldn't show up at all. In the past year she'd been a no-show on quite a few occasions. Initially it pissed Brandon off, but he'd realized he liked not having her around. She was too good at zinging him with one-liners that probably weren't purposely intended to demoralize him, but they did. Long ago he gave up trying to figure out why her remarks had such a profound effect on him. Maybe he simply didn't "get" her. He hoped that didn't happen with Caroline, but so far she was definitely an enigma.

Brandon abruptly stood. *Enough.* Screw the bus. He was going to walk in front of the biggest, fastest-moving vehicle that didn't look like it could stop. Just end it all! What was the point of going on any longer?

Finally, the bus arrived. FINALLY! Was it going by a different time zone? It sure seemed like it. Instead of boarding the bus after about six passengers got off, Brandon remained seated. No one else was waiting to board, so he waved at the driver, who returned the gesture and soon departed. If only there hadn't been glares from every passenger who'd gotten off, Brandon would have felt smug. He was aware that wasn't the appropriate feeling in this case, as he was going to be late for his job at this rate. Even though he hated his current employment, at least it was better than having no job at all. Sort of.

Unfortunately Sandy did show up, right when Brandon was by the water cooler, getting something to drink. It was a popular place for Tip-Top employees to gather, including the ones who brought bottled water. On this particular morning, since the water cooler was on the way to the restrooms, two hotties, Marla and Kristy, came by. Both were newly-employed as secretary/receptionists, and they were eager to stop and chat. Brandon gobbled up the attention and couldn't wait to return it. He was so encouraged by their apparent interest in him, he soon forgot about the embarrassing adhesive strip between his nose and upper lip.

Redheaded Marla couldn't wait too long before proceeding to the restroom, but Kristy, her raven-haired pal, lingered. Soon Brandon managed to have her in stitches after telling a joke that wasn't even very funny, but his delivery of it was undoubtedly what made it so hilarious.

Kristy became so loud with her (forced) laughter, Brandon almost didn't hear the lock turning in the back door, indicating Sandy Messing was arriving. He knew to keep his ears pricked for that "click" sound, his warning she was about to appear! Breezing in the unlocked front entrance wasn't her style; she preferred to be furtive.

The first thing Sandy did was walk right up to Brandon, brushing past Kristy. While zeroing in on "the adhesive strip," she loudly asked, "What in the *hell* did you do to your otherwise handsome self, Mister Burr?"

Brandon didn't immediately respond to the question because he couldn't! He was too embarrassed. However, it did occur to him, his boss was the one who should have felt that. Nonetheless, she somehow "knew" just what to say, to get under his skin. At times he suspected she secretly had a huge crush on him and was in fact a cougar on the prowl. Perhaps it went no deeper than she was in the middle of one of her hangovers, which she handled less well than her various levels of intoxication.

After Kristy finally disappeared to the restroom, Brandon mumbled, "I nicked myself shaving this morning."

Sandy got so close to Brandon, he was certain she was going to plant a kiss on none other than the humiliation-inducing adhesive strip. He did not trust her to do that and then turn right around and accuse him of making a pass at her! All he wanted was to keep his job, and of course that entailed keeping Sandy "happy."

Following that "exchange" with his boss, Brandon didn't even want to leave his cubicle so he didn't. One thing about not taking a lunch break, he could get more done, although the point was to avoid everyone, whether it was Sandy or any hot, new employees.

By five o'clock, however, Brandon was more than ready to go home and chill out in front of the TV. He didn't expect Caroline to cook for him, even if she wasn't quite as busy as she appeared to be. Any spare minutes were devoted to Tippy. Brandon was fine with that; after he relaxed for an hour or two he could order carry-out from someplace and go pick it up. Or maybe Caroline would be up for going out to eat. He really was a pretty easygoing guy.

There was a tap on his shoulder. Brandon had a feeling it was his boss, which made him very uneasy. Since she'd left him alone all day, hopefully the "episode" they shared was long-forgotten. With all she had to do, it should have been the furthest thing from her mind.

Instead, with only the two of them still in the building (that Brandon was aware), Sandy told him, "Brandon. I'd hoped to see you skedaddle off to lunch so I could treat you, though you know I usually stay here for lunch. I feel so horribly about how I must have humiliated you. So since you worked your butt off through the whole day, you deserve a drink on me. You can take me to 'After Five,' and my son will pick me up when he gets off work. We're going to dinner afterward and then he'll bring me back here to get my car."

There did not appear to be any choice in the matter because Sandy refused to remove her hand from his shoulder. He was frankly finding it very annoying, but it was time to stand, which (fortunately) made it impossible for her to keep "a hand on him."

Sandy said, "I'm going to run to the restroom. I'll meet you outside, in front." And that was that.

All Brandon could think was how much he wanted this jaunt to be "quick." Otherwise Caroline would want to know why he smelled like he'd had a drink (on an almost-empty stomach) and was home later than usual. Even though she had Tippy for company, he could already tell there was no predicting what "got to her."

Another bus. Already? Didn't one just stop a couple minutes ago? Maybe he'd been sitting here too long. It almost felt like it would be impossible to get up. What happened? Did Brandon's feet and legs fall asleep? Was he asleep, as in dreaming? No. He was awake, for whatever it was worth.

A woman ran up seemingly out of nowhere to board the bus. The doors had been open, but no one got off. No wonder, given how many buses stopped here. Suddenly Brandon was motivated to get on the bus too, but at this point it seemed like all he could do was blink. But he wasn't about to panic. He didn't care about his new job anyway. There. He admitted the truth.

Driving Sandy to After Five, Brandon was certain she was going to make an audacious pass. When she didn't, he was relieved in a way, but he also felt rejected, of all things! He couldn't believe himself. So he was just as shallow and morally bankrupt as every other guy. As it was, they were pretty close together in his Beetle.

The destination was reached without an incident of any kind, including something driving-related. After a drink with Sandy, Brandon was on his way, whether or not her son had arrived. (There was some sort of pull Sandy exerted, that compelled Brandon to heed her every wish.) It went way beyond "the boss and the kiss-ass employee" dynamic.

Walking into the bar, Brandon was ahead of Sandy, who was busy texting someone, hopefully her son, Wyatt, ordering him to hurry up. It was impossible to imagine her content to stop bossing people around when the work day was done.

"Did you say something?" Sandy asked Brandon as he held the door open for her. Immediately he became nervous, thinking, *Did I move my mouth like I was saying something?* If he did, he really was losing his mind, no two ways about it.

Brandon had never before been in this bar, but he'd heard co-workers rave about the unique and relaxing atmosphere. From the slate-tiled entryway, he already liked the vibe of the place. A rock song was quietly playing in the background, not loudly blasting like at some bars. There was also the pervasive sound of the enormous, rearing, stone Pegasus fountain in the center of the room, where there was also an atrium. The glass ceiling right over the fountain had been retracted, creating an open-air atmosphere. However, the remainder of glass on the ceiling was tinted, so it wasn't as if it was glaringly bright in the bar, even this early in the evening. Nonetheless, Sandy pointed to the leather barstools to the left, beneath a canopy of wood beams, facing a mirrored wall. It was filled with liquor bottles, many of them ornamental. Above them was the only flat-screen TV in the whole place. Since it was still rather early, they had their pick of places to sit, and Brandon wanted to sit at one of the tables for two that encircled the fountain. He even went so far as to remark, "I'll pay for the drinks if we can sit by the fountain." If he sounded like a whiny little kid, too bad! This outing wasn't what he'd wanted to begin with. It was all thanks to that stupid adhesive strip as well as unwanted attention from his boss.

Amazingly, Sandy followed Brandon to a table right by the fountain, one of the most easy to see from the entrance. He didn't go out much, but when he did, he was never concerned with being noticed, even under these particular circumstances. (He still felt as if he were being coerced.) As it was, Sandy had fun, holding her power over Brandon's head. Rather than have a crush on him, she just wanted to crush him, period. Why did nice, well-meaning people irritate everyone else? There really was no place left in the world for someone like him.

Two laminated drink menus were already at the round, frosted-glass-topped table. Brandon dove right in, studying the list of exotic drinks, and Sandy went back to studying her phone. Either she had the menu memorized or she already knew what she wanted, most likely something plain and simple, maybe even straight booze on the rocks. Brandon winced at the mere thought. If she did have a drinking problem, it was to help her put up with herself. That "observation" made Brandon feel terrible! Good thing Sandy couldn't read minds.

A cute waitress in tight, silver Capri pants and a silver-sequined midriff arrived to take their order, first placing a rattan basket of buttery breadsticks on the table. Brandon

Amy Kristoff

was so hungry he could hardly keep from grabbing one and immediately eating the whole thing. Nonetheless, he managed to restrain himself.

Sure enough, Sandy ordered brandy on the rocks. Brandon decided on a "Fudge-a-Liquorious," with three different kinds of alcohol, topped with whipped cream and a Hershey's kiss! There probably wasn't even a hint of the taste of booze in it.

Drinks ordered, Sandy finally put her phone down so she could have one of the delicious-looking breadsticks (so Brandon did, too). After quickly eating it, she sat back and declared, "Brandon, I invited you here because I wanted to formally apologize for how I behaved earlier, singling you out and all that. I don't even remember what it was about."

Fortunately, Brandon had been able to remove the adhesive strip about one in the afternoon, so he wasn't still wearing the reminder of unprecedented humiliation. Meanwhile, he found it entirely impossible to believe Sandy had no recollection of what she'd picked on him about. Whatever the case, he forgave her for humiliating him, as she clearly felt badly about it. *He* didn't need to have alcohol to profess that.

The waitress soon brought the drinks. Just as Brandon was about to take a much-anticipated sip of his "fudge-a-whatever," Sandy proposed a toast to "many more years together." She also said, "I hope we can do this again soon, Brandon. I really enjoy your company." Her drink glass was raised by this time, but right before it touched Brandon's, it sounded as if someone were taking a picture! Who had appeared but Sandy's son, Wyatt, which shouldn't have surprised either she or Brandon. More than ever Brandon wanted to get away from this place, although "the damage" was already done.

However, Brandon knew he was mostly dealing with "remaining employed," so he couldn't simply take off. *Fine.* He'd be introduced to Wyatt Messing and *then* be on his way. If Sandy didn't want him paying for the drinks, all she had to

128

do was speak up, which she was more than capable of doing. Anyway, Wyatt was quite a bit shorter than Brandon, but he was much better-looking and had short, straight, light-blond hair—versus Brandon's longer and curlier, dark-brown hair. Practically polar opposites in build, Wyatt looked like he lifted weights in his spare time.

Brandon was so busy comparing Sandy's son to himself, he didn't even hear Sandy introducing the two of them until she said, "Wyatt, Brandon Burr is my most devoted employee at Tip-Top. I can't get over how well he listens, much better than my Jack Russell, Spitfire!" Even though she laughed at her "joke," no one else did. Maybe Wyatt wasn't so bad, after all. As it was, if Sandy only knew what Brandon thought of dogs.

Anyway, thank goodness for automatic reflexes because that was what Brandon used to stand up and shake hands with Wyatt Messing. It was maddening to be so distracted. What was it about Sandy's son, that got to Brandon? Maybe it was how confident yet laid-back he seemed. That was maddening too. Brandon really needed to get out of here.

Definitely worth noting was the fact Sandy's face lit up when she was around her son. It was endearing in a way, but given her overall demeanor, you had to wonder who "the real Sandy" was. If nothing else, Brandon was made more aware than ever how unpredictable she was.

Finally some peace. A bus hadn't stopped here for a few minutes or even longer. Lately Brandon had been having trouble keeping track of time. Although he was wearing his watch, he couldn't get himself to look at it because doing so reminded him of how he "used to be"—someone who was fanatical about making constructive use of his time, as well as being on time for work, appointments, etc. At this point, all he wanted to do was sit at the bus stop and BE LATE FOR EVERYTHING FOR THE REST OF HIS LIFE.

Amy Kristoff

Never one to speed, Brandon set a new precedent by doing so on the way back to Caroline's (and Brandon's?) apartment, upon leaving Sandy and Wyatt at the bar. The compulsion to return "home," was practically overwhelming.

Caroline opened the front door the second Brandon parked his Beetle under the carport, to the right of *her* Beetle. (They did look cute, parked side-by-side.) As he approached the doorway, he noticed Tippy was standing beside Caroline, who was so mad, she pushed the dog away from the doorway using her slippered foot, almost losing it (in more ways than one). This was a whole different side of her, to be taking her anger about something, out on her beloved pooch.

Face-to-face with Brandon, Caroline continued to stand in the doorway, essentially blocking it while loudly asking him, "Did you remember what day it is and that we were going out for an early dinner to celebrate because I have to get up at four-thirty to drive Karen to the airport?"

So humiliated was Brandon by this verbal onslaught, he was actually inclined to get back in his car and leave—forever! As much as he loved Caroline, he couldn't take her apparent disdain for him. She "seemed to be" attracted to him when they were in the sack, but how long would that last? Besides, it would never be enough to make the relationship last "forever."

Rather than stand his ground, Brandon about fell over himself, apologizing for being late and for forgetting all about Caroline's plans for the following morning. He didn't bother mentioning the rest of what he forgot because he was already obviously "in trouble." He honestly couldn't even recall discussing going out to dinner with her for a special occasion. As it was, he only vaguely knew the names of any of Caroline's friends, but evidently one was named Karen. It was definitely news, Caroline had to take her to the airport the following day.

"I'll go get ready," Brandon said, figuring Caroline would

130

finally move out of the way.

"I don't suppose you bothered to make any sort of a reservation, did you," she remarked as he passed by.

"No, I . . ."

Then she waved her hand, saying, "Sorry I asked."

Brandon was relieved—for the time being.

They were going out to dinner – and Brandon was driving Caroline back in the direction of "After Five." He liked the bar so much, he figured they could have a drink there, while Caroline continued to debate where to have her 30th birthday dinner. Meanwhile, *he* was supposed to magically know it was not only her birthday, but her big three-o, etc. Brandon had some time to think after Caroline had lost it on him when he got home, and he was certain she hadn't mentioned most of the stuff she'd accused him of forgetting. The important question was why would she do this? It was bad enough his boss had it in for him. It was impossible they were in cahoots to drive him insane, but it was working anyway.

Ever since Brandon and Caroline got in his Beetle, she'd been doing what else but playing with her phone. Initially he thought she was researching what restaurant they should go to, but the way she kept smiling and then madly punching keys, most likely she was texting someone. Maybe it was her friend Karen, confirming plans for tomorrow morning.

About a mile from After Five, Caroline said, "How about 'Petite Maison'? I don't know why I didn't think of it sooner. And it's just a couple miles straight ahead on Camelback Road. If it's open on Mondays, there's no way it's busy this early, so it won't matter we don't have a reservation."

"It might be busy if everyone thinks like you do," Brandon remarked, not trying to be negative. He dreaded going to what he knew was an expensive restaurant, where he would be paying the bill. He'd never dined there, but he'd heard the food and service were both "worth the price." Although he

131

was curious to find out, he was much more interested in pleasing Caroline—if that was even possible.

Given the lack of vehicles in the parking lot, it appeared they'd practically have the place to themselves. Even though Brandon knew what Sandy drove (a white Toyota Camry), he probably wouldn't have noticed it, were it in the parking lot. She'd arrived with her son in his black Dodge Ram pick-up, so Brandon didn't have "fair warning" regarding their presence, not that it would have made any difference.

The first table right inside the granite-tiled dining room was occupied by none other than Sandy and her son, the former facing the entrance. It was impossible for her not to see everyone who made an appearance. The second she laid eyes on Brandon (behind the hostess and Caroline), she exclaimed, "Brandon! Fancy seeing you here!"

Meanwhile, Wyatt leaped up and couldn't wait to shake hands with Brandon again. Then Brandon had to introduce Caroline to the guy, and she looked like she was drooling while shaking hands with him. Brandon wasn't exactly surprised she was attracted to Wyatt Messing, yet it still didn't seem like the guy was her type. Then again, maybe she didn't have a type. Instead, she got lost in a guy upon first sight and followed her lust, how ever long it lasted, even if it was only twenty-four hours. Whatever the case, Brandon was on borrowed time.

As if "poor" Brandon's head wasn't spinning already, he proceeded to witness (after Wyatt introduced his mother to Caroline) none other than Wyatt, pulling out his phone and enthusiastically showing Caroline a picture of Brandon sharing a toast with Sandy at After Five. Wyatt's comment: "I'm so glad to have this momento of my mother, actually enjoying herself. Thank you, Brandon Burr!"

Despite the shaky start to their evening out, Brandon liked to think Caroline's "birthday dinner" was actually enjoyable once they sat down together. Although Brandon hadn't made any provision for a sing-along and dessert for

Caroline's birthday (he still didn't believe it really was her "big day"), it didn't appear to annoy her. Perhaps she simply got over her initial anger about him "forgetting her day," and she'd accepted his repentance. He was in fact able to explain the circumstances under which he was having a drink with his boss after work, making him late getting home.

The Messings were (fortunately) long gone when Caroline and Brandon left Petite Maison. Returning to her place, Caroline was very much "in the mood." Brandon was so into the moment, his iffy relationship with her was temporarily forgotten. Things got so intense, he ended up leaving his brandy-colored, Spanish calfskin loafers by the sofa in the living room, while his brown dress pants and underwear ended up under the Mexican-crafted coffee table with a glass inlay. Caroline managed to remain dressed until they got to the bedroom.

Around one A.M., Brandon had to get a drink of water, and only a chilled bottled water would do, requiring a trip to the kitchen. He didn't turn on any lights, but he could vaguely see his shoes. Even though he'd intended to get the water first and then worry about his clothes, he wanted to put on the loafers. He was not comfortable walking barefoot around a place where he already had a mishap. Leaning over, he suddenly smelled "poop," and it was in his left shoe! Hell. Left, right, what did it matter? The bottom line was that cretinous #@!* of a dog did that for one reason, and it wasn't because Caroline neglected to take the animal out upon their return from the b-day dinner (although he would later be blamed for "distracting her" when they got home). That dog hated Brandon and resented his mere presence (let alone whatever else he provided Caroline beyond what a dog could offer).

As much as Brandon did not want to "lose it" by taking his anger out on that damnable dog, he was too incensed to care. The unsoiled loafer in hand, he went in search of Tippy, who was probably in her bed, by the washer and dryer. Why the dog wasn't contained in there by a gate or barrier of some sort was beyond Brandon. However, he did recall Caroline alluding to occasionally letting her furry friend "join her in bed" if the dog meandered into her bedroom in the middle of the night. Fortunately Tippy hadn't attempted that while Brandon had been occupying the bed. There was only room for two people in that queen-sized bed, as far as he was concerned.

Discipline was in order for that damned dog, and Brandon was about to dispense as much to that unrepentant shit. It was asleep (or appeared to be), so the first couple whacks with the shoe would likely elicit some loud yelps. Brandon felt terrible about it, but he actually looked forward to hearing what noise the dog made.

Just as he predicted, Brandon surprised the hell out of Tippy, upon first hitting the dog on its butt. Tippy initially yelped as if shocked, and following the second hit, cried as if in extreme pain. Then he turned on a light to get a better look at his "target."

"You faker!" Brandon hissed. "I did not hit you hard enough to cause you any pain. But I could, you bitch! Here! Take this!" and whacked the dog a third time.

Brandon about jumped out of his skin when from behind him Caroline exclaimed, "That's enough! Enough!" He turned around to witness her standing in her floor-length, aqua-colored terrycloth robe, tears streaming down her face, which looked completely distraught. "I know you aren't exactly a dog-person, and you barely know Tippy, but I had expected you'd at least give her a chance. What am I supposed to think of you?" Then she burst into tears and ran to the bedroom, slamming the door behind her. He assumed there was a lock on it, but he wasn't about to find out if it did (or if it was locked).

Seconds later the door flew open and Caroline reappeared with a navy blue fleece blanket and a pillow without a pillowcase. "Here!" she said and threw them both at him, as he was back to standing by the sofa, feeling like a total idiot.

If nothing else, Tippy wasn't going anywhere for the evening, meaning she was remaining in her bed by the washer and dryer. Obviously Caroline wasn't too worried about the dog making yet another mess. Or maybe she figured Tippy could just shit in Brandon's other shoe and be done with it.

Somehow Brandon got up in time for work, but he felt (appropriately) like crap. The last thing he wanted to face after a long day at work was that pair of ruined (and expensive) shoes, so he'd toss them in the trash collection area at the rear of the apartment complex before leaving for the day.

If Caroline took Karen to the airport, she must have decided to take Tippy with her and go straight to work afterward. Maybe all this was a good thing. Some time away from Brandon would give Caroline a chance to cool off. It was imperative to be realistic about the odds of them having a lasting relationship. He liked to think that overall, he was reasonably practical-minded, but regarding Caroline, he was unrealistic. Apparently he couldn't admit defeat when it came to "making" Caroline fall in love with him. Getting caught red-handed disciplining her dog, didn't help (despite the fact the animal deserved it). To Caroline it was "just a pair of shoes Tippy ruined," although it was obvious they weren't cheap. Some monetary compensation would have been appreciated but was never going to materialize. As it stood, he figured he'd be getting kicked out by the end of the day. Nonetheless, he held out the hope, she'd realize how loyal he was and let him stick around.

Everyone at Tip-Top left for lunch. Good. It never used to bother Brandon whether he had the place to himself or not, but suddenly he wanted to be alone in the worst way. Was he preparing himself for his break-up with Caroline, later in the day? He wished he didn't care so much about losing her.

Nonetheless, he had no regrets about having "helped matters" by disciplining her dog and having her witness it.

During the work day, Brandon wasn't supposed to take (or make) personal calls on his phone, but he could on breaks or during his lunch hour. His phone was indeed on, but he was busy on his computer, searching for an available apartment (preferably one he could move into right away). Otherwise he would have to do some couch-surfing for a few days.

Then Caroline called. Brandon thought he found a rental and was ready to "move on" (but not really). She greeted him warmly and said, "Guess what I just did?"

"I can't imagine."

"I had lunch with your boss, Sandra Messing! She is a hoot! It must be the gin martini she has every day. I don't know how she does it."

Obviously Caroline hadn't been around much, given how in awe she was of Brandon's drunkard of a boss. Could it get any worse?

"So how did that invite come about?" Brandon just had to ask, curiosity literally killing him.

"She called me out of the blue about ten-thirty, inviting me to lunch. I was just going to head home and grab a bite. She asked if it was all right if her son joined us. Of course I said it was O.K., only because I thought it would help you look good."

Brandon could not believe Caroline was serious. Hopefully she didn't take him for being *that* dumb. It was plain as day she couldn't wait to spend some time with Wyatt Messing, even if doing so included her future mother-in-law, who was playing matchmaker.

"What about Tippy?" Brandon asked, risking having Caroline get sarcastic with him. "She wasn't around when I left for work."

"She's at the vet for grooming and vaccinations, like a doggie day spa," Caroline replied. "She sheds a lot so I have her clipped short a couple times a year."

It was a huge relief for Brandon not to hear: "Why would *you* give a shit about Tippy?" Not only that, Caroline was being sweet—way too sweet. That bothered him more than anything. Rather than finding an apartment he had something else he'd much rather do.

"So where are you now?" Brandon asked.

"I'm driving back to work," Caroline replied. "But I get off at two-thirty, so I'll be able to pick up Tippy well before they close at five."

Brandon wanted to say, "I'll see you when you get home from work," but he figured he'd be home well before that. Maybe he was losing his mind, making it difficult to be rational, but he was compelled to go through with the "something else" he was suddenly obsessed with. Doing so would undoubtedly get him fired and make it almost impossible to get another job. With that, he went in Sandy's office and plopped down in her overstuffed, burgundy leather swivel chair. She liked to boast she "usually" stayed here for lunch, but the truth of the matter was she often "barely arrived" for the work day and left again—for lunch! She probably hadn't yet eaten because she awoke late and was too hung over to have breakfast.

After removing his cheap, black, faux-leather loafers, Brandon propped his feet up on the desk. The only reason he took them off was so he didn't have to gaze at a pair of crappy-looking shoes. He sure as shit didn't care about getting his dirty loafers on his selfish boss' fancy oak desk. Given Brandon's sleepless night, it wasn't any wonder he proceeded to fall asleep.

Finally someone called 911, to bring an ambulance for "a guy who's sitting up at a bus stop bench like he's waiting to go to work but looks pretty much dead." Somehow the issue of *Man World* he'd been reading, ended up under his left shoe—a cheap-looking, navy docksider. At least Brandon

Amy Kristoff

Burr hadn't felt any pain, other than from a broken heart.

6/4/24

Amy has written several novels and short story collections, including *Retribution and Other Twisted Tales*, in 2016. She resides on a horse farm in Indiana. AmyKristoff.com.

CPSIA information can be obtained
at www.ICGtesting.com
Printed in the USA
FSOW02n0821180517
34145FS